THE HAPPILY EVER AFTER
BOOKSTORE

BERNADETTE MARIE

5 Prince Publishing

Published by 5 PRINCE PUBLISHING & BOOKS, LLC

PO Box 865, Arvada, CO 80001

www.5PrinceBooks.com

ISBN digital: 978-1-63112-283-5

ISBN print: 978-1-63112-284-2

Cover Credit: Marianne Nowicki

To Stan,

Sometimes you meet someone in August,
fall in love in October,
and are engaged by January.

Lucky me.

Thank you for being my Happily Ever After.

ACKNOWLEDGMENTS

To my boys, I hope you find your happily ever after, no matter what that might look like to you. You deserve happiness, always.

To my Mama and Sissy, How lucky am I to get family and friends? Yeah, we could totally be in business together—haha. Though it would be a quilt store with a book section.

To Cate, Meh! (I love you!) Thank you for your knowledge and your humor.

To Ronda Simmons, thanks for the book and the fun inspiration! Potatoes for all! Check out her book: The Potato Primer.

To Kari Horst, Barbara Hackel, Mindy Berkner, Megan Hammond, and Carissa Robins—Thank you for taking the time to be the last set of eyes on this fun project. I appreciate you!

To my Dedicated and Valued Readers, Thank you for coming back time after time to fall in love with characters that are near and dear to my heart.

OTHER TITLES BY BERNADETTE MARIE

Date for Hire

THE DEVEREAUX FAMILY SERIES

Kennedy Devereaux

Chase Devereaux

Max Devereaux

Paige Devereaux

FUNERALS AND WEDDINGS SERIES

Something Lost

Something Discovered

Something Found

Something Forbidden

Something New

STAND ALONE TITLES

The Happily Ever After Bookstore

THE HAPPILY EVER AFTER
BOOKSTORE

PART I
THE BOOK SWAP

CHAPTER 1

BELLS CHIMED ABOVE THE DOOR AS SADIE PUSHED IT OPEN AND walked into the bookstore. The smell of books, old and new, incense, teas, and soaps filled her nose.

It had been cold enough outside that when she stepped into the warm store, her glasses fogged up.

Slipping them off, she wiped them with the ends of her scarf, and put them back on.

Sadie had been coming to the bookstore since high school. Leona, the bookstore owner, was a whimsical woman whom Sadie enjoyed. On her recommendation, Sadie read all the great classics, such as *The Great Gatsby, Catcher in the Rye, Romeo and Juliet*.

Leona was the first person to hand her a copy of *Harry Potter*. As she grew older, Sadie's tastes changed quite a bit. Now, she rather enjoyed a contemporary romance that offered a happily ever after.

She wasn't above reading a great mystery or science-fiction novel, Sadie found that she just enjoyed people falling in love.

Perhaps she enjoyed it as much as she did, now that she was edging out of her twenties, because she had yet to find love

3

herself. Her mother had never found love, not even with Sadie's father. But that wasn't unusual, many of Sadie's friends' parents were not married either. It was a sign of the times. Things were hard. Money was tight. And, sometimes, people just didn't care about one another after a while.

Leona appeared from behind the bookshelf. Her wiry long hair, which was never colored and now glinted with strands of silver, hung past her shoulders, and the many bangle bracelets on her wrist jingled.

"Sadie, my darling, how are you today?" Leona asked.

Sadie hiked her purse up on her shoulder. "I am wonderful. How are you?"

Leona waved her hands through the air, as she would often do, to encompass the store. "Everything is perfect. What have you come in for today? A new fantasy? I have one that will take you through the forest with fae. I have a new biography; of a silver screen legend. Oh, and I have a cookbook for you, or for your mother, so you can use all of those potatoes you have." Leona smiled.

Sadie couldn't help but smile at the comment. That summer, Sadie had purchased a book for her mother on gardening. It seemed as if all of a sudden the earth was speaking to Sadie's mother, and she wanted to garden. As it was, the only thing her mother was handy at growing was potatoes.

"I may have to look at the potato book after all. But I was thinking I would love a holiday romance."

Leona gave a low hum in consideration. "A holiday romance? The holidays are almost over."

Sadie nodded. "Yes, but I'm needing something to make me feel more festive, I suppose. Tomorrow is Christmas Eve, and my mom is so depressed, she didn't want me to help her put up the tree or any lights this year. So I need some happily ever after."

Leona's forehead creased as she thought. "Go back to the

romance section. Let me check my computer," she said, lifting her brows in encouragement as the front door chimed again.

Sadie walked to the section on romance, which she was more than familiar with.

Leona had shelves of new books and used books. Some of them Sadie had already read and brought back for store credit. But she looked at the spine of each book and knew buried in the pages were love stories which brought her hope.

CHARLIE WINCED AT THE SMELL OF THE SMALL STORE WHEN HE walked in. Even his grandmother didn't wear that many scents at one time. What was all of that?

He'd considered turning around, but the woman who moved in behind the counter had already caught his eye.

She smiled wide, her piercing blue eyes sparkling from six feet away. When she moved about behind the counter, her bracelets clanked together. Pushing her hair over her shoulder, she picked up a teacup from a saucer and lifted it to her lips.

"Hello, how are you today?" she asked.

Charlie felt a warmth resonate from her greeting, and he thought it was funny because a moment earlier he'd been freezing outside.

"Good, thanks." He pulled off his gloves and continued to walk into the store.

"Are you looking for anything specific?" the woman asked.

Charlie pulled off his hat and assumed his hair had sprung up when the woman's eyes lifted. "I suppose I am. I'm looking for a book about some old movie star that just came out. I don't know. The cover is white, and the image is in black and white."

The woman smiled wide. "I know exactly which one you're looking for. It's three shelves over and facing out. You can't miss it."

Charlie nodded, tucking his cap and gloves into the pocket of his coat.

He walked toward the section where the woman had directed him. A woman bundled in a coat and scarf looked at the shelves on the adjacent wall. Eventually, they were nearly back-to-back, each searching for books.

The woman had been right. When he saw the book, he knew it right away. Charlie took it from the shelf and stepped back just as the woman behind him did the same.

The woman stumbled one way, dropping her book, he stumbled the other direction, dropping his.

"I'm so sorry," the woman said as she scrambled to pick up both books. As she rose, the book he'd come for in her hand, Charlie blinked hard.

The woman holding out the book to him looked as if she'd walked out of a cartoon illustration of a bookworm. Of course, she was real, and cute. Big round glasses accentuated large dark eyes. There were freckles on her nose, and her curly hair was piled atop her head in a very messy bun.

Charlie wasn't sure why he couldn't even speak.

"Vivian Leigh?" she asked, looking down at the book. "Are you an old movie buff?"

Charlie blinked again, realizing she was talking to him. "No."

"Oh," the woman said, her pink lips forming that O long after the words had vanished. "I wonder if this was the book Leona was telling me about." She turned it over and looked at the back.

"Who is Leona?" he asked.

"The woman who owns the store."

"I told her what the cover of the book I was in search of looked like. She told me where to find it."

The woman, still holding out the book he'd dropped, smiled. "She's a book miracle. She knows every book and every story in this store." The woman looked again at the book in her hand. "But this wasn't the one you wanted?"

Charlie finally took the book from her. "No, well yes, it was. It's not for me. It's for my grandmother. She has Alzheimer's. She doesn't remember any of us, but she remembers these people," he said, looking at the cover of the book and then wondering why he'd shared that much information.

"I think she'll enjoy it then."

Charlie nodded and watched as the woman turned and walked away.

Looking down at the book and then back up at the empty space where the woman had been, he wondered why he felt so odd. Maybe it was all the scents in the store, and they were just making him dizzy.

CHAPTER 2

"I THINK I FOUND ONE," SADIE SAID AS SHE HANDED THE BOOK TO Leona.

"Oh, I like this one. You made a wise choice," Leona said as the man who had bumped into Sadie walked up behind her.

Leona lifted her head to acknowledge the man. "You found it."

"Yeah," he said. "I knew it when I saw it. Just like you'd said."

Leona took the book from him. "Let me get it wrapped up for you. It's a Christmas gift, correct?"

The man nodded and the mass of blond curls atop his head bounced as he did so. "For my grandmother."

Leona picked up Sadie's book as well. "Let me wrap these up for you both, and we'll get you on your way."

Leona carried the books to a counter behind the cash register and turned her back to them.

The man leaned closer to Sadie. "She's really wrapping them?"

Sadie nodded. "She wraps everything. It doesn't matter what it is. She believes that if you buy it for yourself, it's a gift too."

The man nodded slowly and eased back.

When Leona turned around, she had two books wrapped in

Christmas paper. She slid them into brown craft bags with the bookstore's name stamped on the front.

Leona rang up the two sales and gave each of them their totals.

Sadie began to dig through her purse and the man handed Leona his credit card.

"Actually, why don't you put both books on my card," he offered, and Sadie snapped her head.

"You don't have to do that."

The corners of the man's mouth curled up. "I feel like it. I don't know what it is about this store, but it makes me feel Christmassy."

Sadie looked around. Leona had added a few lights and that antique aluminum silver tree in the window. Maybe it was festive among the clutter.

"Are you sure? You don't know me."

The man nodded and held out his hand. "I'm Charlie."

Sadie shook his hand, though she still had her fingerless mittens on. "Sadie."

"Now I know you," Charlie said as Leona handed him both bags. "Merry Christmas, Sadie." He handed her the bag.

"Merry Christmas, Charlie."

Charlie looked back at Leona. "Merry Christmas to you, too. My grandmother is going to love her book."

Leona pressed her hands together at her chest, as if in prayer, and smiled at Charlie. "Merry Christmas. I'm sure the book will make you very happy," Leona said with a wink.

Charlie waited for Leona to realize what she'd said, but she kept smiling at him, as if they shared some secret. Charlie decided that was his signal to leave, and he gave them both a little wave, and walked out of the store.

Sadie watched him until he had disappeared before she turned back to Leona. "Have you ever seen him before?"

Leona shook her head. "No. He's a new soul in my store. He's very kind and loves his family."

Sadie narrowed her eyes on Leona. "How do you know that?"

Leona raised her finger and her bangles jingled. "I talked to him about his grandmother, whom he's very fond of. And, you can see his kind heart. It comes through in his eyes. He'll be a good friend to have. He's a little sad. I'm going to assume that has something to do with his grandmother."

Nodding, Sadie lifted her purse onto her shoulder again. "He said his grandmother has Alzheimer's and only remembers the actresses in the old movies."

Placing her hands flat on the counter, Leona drew in a deep breath. "See, he will be a kind and good friend."

Smiling, Sadie picked up her bag with the gifted book. Leona always made her feel happy, but Sadie often wondered how much of what Leona said was just a sales tactic.

It didn't matter. Sadie would always be back in the bookstore buying books or gifts. The energy in the store was a happy one, and Sadie could regularly use that shot of positivity.

～

CHARLIE WALKED THE TWELVE BLOCKS FROM THE *HAPPILY EVER After Bookstore* to his grandmother's care facility. He wasn't sure if he'd get to see her on Christmas Eve or Christmas. He wasn't even sure she knew it was Christmas.

As he pulled open the door to walk inside, he held his breath. The scent always made him a little nauseous. Immediately, his thoughts went back to the bookstore and the mix of scents he'd walked into there. He'd take that blast to the senses over this one any day.

"Hey, Charlie," the nurse at the station said as he walked in. "Here to see your Grandma?"

Charlie nodded. "I am."

"Your dad came by a while ago. Poked his head in and went back out," she said on a disappointed sigh.

"He struggles with it."

"I know. Did you bring her something?"

Charlie looked down at the bag in his hand. "I did. She talked about a book about an actress the last time I was here. She didn't talk to me about it as much as she was placing an order for it."

The nurse nodded her understanding. "They'll do that."

"Anyway, I told the woman at the store what I was looking for and here it is. She might not understand why I brought it, but she'll have it."

"You're a good grandson," the nurse said before she took a call.

Charlie walked down the hall to his grandmother's room.

His grandmother sat in the recliner next to her bed. Her silver hair had been combed and someone had brought her a small plant that had Christmas decorations on it. She hadn't seen him walk in because she was watching the lights twinkle on the plant.

"Hey, Grandma," Charlie said softly as to not startle her.

Her crystal blue eyes, which were always clear, shifted to look at him, but she didn't speak.

"I brought you a gift. You'd mentioned that there was a book you would like," he said, pulling the wrapped book from the bag he carried. "You had explained it to me and the woman at the store knew exactly which book it was."

Charlie handed her the book and noticed that her fingernails had been polished too. He was grateful to whoever had taken such good care of her to make sure she looked pretty and had nice things.

His grandmother took the wrapped book, studied it, and held it to her chest as if she already cherished it.

"You can pull off the paper," he said.

His grandmother studied the gift again, then gingerly, and slowly, she began to tear the wrapping off.

Charlie took off his commuter bag and set it on the floor before pulling off his hat and gloves, tucking them into his coat pocket. He shrugged out of his coat and draped it over the foot of her bed. Sitting down on the edge of her bed, he watched as his grandmother took her time unwrapping the book.

Eventually, the paper was removed.

Charlie's grandmother ran her fingers over the cover and a smile came to her lips. When she lifted it to her chest to hold it close, Charlie noticed the front cover.

Romancing Christmas, the title said.

The woman at the bookstore had mixed up the books.

CHAPTER 3

SADIE HELD THE BOOK IN HER HANDS. HOW DID THAT HAPPEN?

With her legs crossed beneath her, seated in the middle of her bed, she picked up the brown craft bag that Leona had put her book in and checked to make sure it had been the only thing inside.

She looked at the biography of Vivian Leigh. Though it had been one of the books which Leona had suggested for her, she knew that it was supposed to be a thoughtful gift for a grand-mother who didn't remember anyone but the people in old movies.

Certainly, Charlie had made it out of the store with her romance novel.

Perhaps his grandmother would enjoy it, but guilt plagued her. The woman knew Vivian Leigh—did she even know Charlie?

Gently opening the book, Sadie read the front cover, then she flipped the pages.

With her fuzzy slippers and her cozy sweater to keep her warm, she continued to turn the pages of the biography gently, absorbing all the juicy details of the silver screen legend's life.

Tomorrow she would take the book to Leona with the purpose of getting it back to Charlie, regardless of whether she got her book back. After all, he'd paid for both of them.

Hours later, when she'd finished the biography, she folded the wrapping paper back around it and placed it in the bag.

Biographies were always interesting, Sadie thought. Someday, if someone were going to write about her, would they have anything to say?

Sadie climbed off her bed and set the bag with the book by the door, so she could remember to take it with her tomorrow.

Walking to her small kitchenette, Sadie pulled a mug from her cabinet and filled it with water. Opening the microwave door, she tucked the mug inside, closed the door, and hit the power. As her water warmed, she looked out the window and down on to the street below.

Christmas filled the streets, and for that she was grateful. Her apartment was so small, the only tree she had was one that sat on the top of her nightstand next to her bed, which doubled as her couch. She'd made origami ornaments for it over the years, and also strung up garland across the windows with origami shapes and popcorn.

But below her, the world sparkled. Stores displayed beautiful windows. The trees were wrapped in lights. Scents from the bakery and the chestnut vendor rose and seeped through tiny gaps in her windows. The coffee shop in the unit below her apartment, smelled of fresh coffee each morning when she woke.

From her window, she could see Leona's store a few blocks away.

People walked up and down the quaint street, and carolers sang on the corners.

Usually, she wasn't sad during Christmas. Surrounded by so much joy, it was hard to be anything less. But her mother's mood had rubbed off on her, and wasn't it funny that she thought of Charlie's grandmother and that made her sad too.

At the rate that Sadie was going, she'd never have a grandchild who loved her enough to buy her books, whether she knew their names at her advanced age or not. The thought saddened her even more.

Opening the window to the chill outside, she listened to the bells on the carriages that went up and down the street, and enjoyed the songs that were being sung.

It would all go back to normal in a few days. But for that moment, she was going to make the most of the joyful noise.

∾

CHARLIE DECIDED TO STOP BY AND SEE HIS GRANDMOTHER AGAIN on Christmas Eve morning. If she wasn't still attached to the book he'd brought her, he'd sneak it out and take it back to the bookstore.

When he walked into his grandmother's room, she lifted her eyes to him and smiled.

"Good morning, handsome," she said clearly.

Charlie stepped back out the door, looked at the name on the nameplate next to the room number, and then walked back in. His grandmother never acknowledged him like that—or sometimes at all.

"Hello, Grandma," he said carefully as he walked toward her, his coat still buttoned, gloves on, and his scarf wrapped around his neck. "How are you today?"

"I'm wonderful. Your father was here earlier," she said, but Charlie wasn't so sure about that. He'd talked to his father, and there had been no mention of him visiting. "Your grandfather came by too," she said, and then Charlie knew she was delusional. His grandfather had died when Charlie was ten.

"Is that so?" he asked as he began to unwind the scarf. "It sounds as if you had a busy morning."

"Sit down. Sit down," she demanded in her grandmotherly

tone, which he hadn't heard in years. In fact, it nearly brought him to tears. "Is it cold outside?"

Charlie nodded as he sat on the edge of her bed, so he could face his grandmother in her recliner. "Have you had your breakfast?"

"I did. They brought us a special breakfast. It's Christmas Eve, you know."

Charlie's chest tightened. "I do know."

His grandmother turned toward the small table at her side. Just as it had when she lived in her own home, the table-top was filled with newspapers, crossword puzzle books, a cup with pencils, hand lotion, and her glasses.

From the top of the pile of puzzle books and newspapers, she picked up the book he'd given her and handed it to him.

"Thank you for the book, Charlie," she called him by name and Charlie bit down on his lip to keep it from trembling. "It was so wonderful. I want you to read it now."

Charlie took the book from his grandmother and looked down at it. *Romancing Christmas*, was the title. On the cover was an illustration of a couple leaned in toward one another, and the girl was carrying a book, which was pressed to her chest. The man, he noticed, had what appeared to be a mop of curly blond hair just like his own.

Lifting his eyes to meet his grandmother's, Charlie noted how she appeared to be fully engaged in what she was telling him. Her eyes were locked on him as he'd looked at the book.

"You want me to read a romance book?" he asked.

His grandmother nodded, and then took his hand. "Fall in love, Charlie," she said using his name and now his eyes did well up with tears. "She's out there waiting."

CHAPTER 4

Sadie hurried down the small street between her apartment and Leona's bookstore. The festiveness of Christmas had doubled, she thought, as people walked in and out of stores with cups of drinks, which she didn't know if they were coffee or cocoa. Music played from every doorway, and the scents of chestnuts at ten in the morning nearly overwhelmed her.

Did all of these people wait until the last moment to shop? Or, because it was a Saturday morning, and Christmas Eve, were they all just feeling festive and wanting to mingle?

When Sadie pushed open the door to the bookstore, she could smell the cinnamon candles that Leona would burn. People walked around the store picking up books and gift items. There was a hum of conversation and the meditation music drowned out the Christmas music from the street.

In all the years that Sadie had been walking into the store, she'd never seen it quite like this.

Leona, lifted her head to see her walk in. There was a line in front of the counter, and by Leona's smile, she was very happy to have her store so full.

Sadie reconsidered her reason for being there. Leona didn't have time to worry about the mistaken book.

Sadie walked toward the counter. "Good morning, Leona."

"Hello, sweetheart," she said, smiling at her, but continuing to ring up customers. "It's a beautiful day, isn't it?"

"You're very busy."

"Holidays on the weekend are miracles," she nearly sang the words as she thanked the couple at the counter and handed them their bag before the next customer walked up. "Are you in need of another book already?" she asked, and Sadie only shrugged.

There was no way she was going to tell her about the mix-up now. Not that Leona wouldn't make it right, but that she was much too busy.

"I just wanted to stop in and say hello," Sadie said. "I'll stop back by when you're not so busy."

"Enjoy your day, sweetheart," Leona said as she rang up the next sale. "And if I don't see you, Merry Christmas."

Sadie gave her a wave, and then maneuvered through the crowd and out of the bookstore.

As she stood on the street, Sadie wondered if she could find Charlie on her own. Did he work close by? Was his grandmother in a facility close by?

Seriously, it wasn't a priority. She could take the book back to the store, and if Charlie wandered in, Leona could get in touch with her.

Pulling her phone from her pocket, and walking against the flow of pedestrian traffic, she began to search for care facilities near her. Perhaps Charlie's grandmother was in one, or she lived at home, but what would it hurt to look?

Then again, what was she going to do, walk into the facility and ask if they had a woman who had a grandson named Charlie?

Chuckling to herself at the absurdity of the thought, she nearly dropped her phone when a shoulder of a passerby bumped into her. She stopped and turned, just as the man who had bumped her turned.

Sadie felt her mouth open, and she stared at the man whom she was on a quest to find.

CHARLIE SWALLOWED HARD AS HE LOOKED AT THE WOMAN FROM the bookstore. "I'm sorry. I didn't mean to—"

"It's okay," she said.

Then, at the same time, they both said, "I was looking for you."

The woman's eyes went wide.

God, he wished he could remember her name. "You were looking for me?" Charlie asked.

The woman nodded as she dug into her oversized purse. "Leona got the books switched yesterday. I wanted to make sure your grandmother got the right book."

Charlie blinked hard. "I know the books were mixed up, but you were out here looking for me?"

She nodded. "I was just looking for care facilities in the area. I thought maybe you were with your Grandmother today. I didn't know how to ask anyone about Charlie's grandmother, but..."

Charlie stepped closer to her. "You remember my name?"

"I always remember names."

"I don't. Tell me yours again."

When she smiled, a dimple formed in her cheek. "Sadie."

"That's right," he said, knowing he'd never forget it again. "Sadie," he repeated as another man bumped into him.

"Take it somewhere else. You're in the way," the man growled as he walked on.

Sadie pursed her lips. "I guess not everyone has the holiday spirit."

"Are you in a hurry to get somewhere?" Charlie asked.

Sadie shook her head. "No."

"Can I buy you a cup of coffee or hot chocolate?"

"Oh," she said, tapping her fingers on the book with Vivian Leigh's face. "I'm sure you have a million things going on today. Family and Christmas and all."

Charlie shook his head. "Not until this evening. I'd love to talk to you about the book you picked out."

Sadie's brows rose. "You read the book?"

"No, but my grandmother did."

"She likes romances? I have an entire bookshelf of them I could let her read."

There was an urgency in him now to sit down with this woman and get to know her. He'd never read a romance in his life, nor did he know anything about them. What he knew was that for the first time in years, his grandmother remembered his name. Maybe those books were magic.

"Really, can I buy you a coffee? I'd really like to talk to—I mean if you're not rushing off for Christmas Eve festivities or family events yourself."

He noticed her eyes flashed sadness.

"No, I have nowhere to go."

"I work in the coffee shop down the street. I can get us anything. I know for a fact they baked fresh chocolate chip muffins. Usually, on Saturdays they use what was frozen during the week. And I probably shouldn't tell people that. It sounds bad, but most of the coffee shops around use frozen items."

Sadie laughed. He'd certainly talked too much, which he did when he was nervous.

Still smiling, she rested her hand on his arm. "I would love a latte."

CHAPTER 5

SADIE FOLLOWED CHARLIE DOWN THE STREET TO THE COFFEE SHOP.
When they crossed the street, she chuckled to herself, but it must
have been loud enough that it caused Charlie to turn to look
at her.

"What's funny?" he asked.

"That you work here."

"I've worked here for three years. It's good hours while I
finish my master's degree."

Didn't that say a lot about the man? "I've never seen you here,"
Sadie admitted. "I live upstairs."

Charlie's eyes went wide. "I live upstairs," he said.

Now they both laughed. How hadn't they ever crossed paths
before the day they'd run into one another at Leona's?

"2B," Sadie admitted and then wondered if she should have.
What if he was just fishing for information, and now he knew
where she lived.

"3C. I have a view of the dumpster in the alley."

Well, at least she knew that to be true. Maybe he did in fact
live on the floor above her.

Charlie pulled open the door to the coffee house. "I hope I'll see you around more often now that we know we each frequent this area," he said with a laugh.

Sadie nodded as she stepped into the quaint coffee shop which she visited often.

CHARLIE LOOKED AROUND THE COFFEE HOUSE. CHRISTMAS EVE WAS fairly busy. How had he managed the day off, he wondered.

The tables and the high bar were all filled. But at that moment, two people stood and vacated the small table tucked in the corner.

He pointed. "Go take those seats. I'll go behind the counter and make our drinks. Do you like chocolate chip?"

Sadie nodded.

"I'll bring us muffins," he offered.

As Charlie slid behind the counter, Sadie hurried to the table to claim their seats. Everyone said hello to him as he moved in behind them and began to make their lattes.

"How did you get the day off?" Allison asked as she shifted over so that he could use the milk.

"I was just wondering that myself. Now I feel like I should have stayed away. You guys are really busy. I don't want to get stuck here."

Allison shook her head. "You won't. I don't know how you got out of it, but we're overstaffed. We have plenty of people today." She put the lid on the drink she'd been working on and set it on the counter. She called out the name on the cup and went about making the next drink. "Who did you come in with?" Allison asked.

"Her name is Sadie."

"I've never seen you on a date before."

Charlie shook his head and felt his mouth go dry. "I'm not on a date."

"Oh, is she a cousin?"

"What? No. We just met."

Allison giggled. "Is she homeless, and you're feeding her?"

"No." He realized he was flustered now for no reason. "I met her at the bookstore. Our books got switched. My grandma read her book and called me by name," he rattled out.

Allison called out another name and put the coffee she'd created on the counter as he fumbled with his own.

"Dude, you're talking in circles. I can't wait to understand what the heck you're really saying, but get your drinks and get over there. She's super cute behind those big ole' glasses," Allison said with a wink.

Charlie lifted his eyes to look over the counter at Sadie, who pulled off her gloves and hat, tucking them into the pockets of her coat.

Yeah, he thought as he looked across the store at her, she was super cute.

Sadie settled in at the table. The store was busier than she'd ever remembered seeing it. As she looked around, she realized she recognized everyone behind the counter as someone she'd interacted with, everyone but Charlie.

But he moved between stations as if he did it every day. Those around him talked to him, so obviously they knew who he was. How was it that they lived in the same building, and he worked in the same coffee shop she visited, yet she'd never crossed his path until yesterday?

A few minutes later, Charlie walked toward her with a tray in one hand and a bag in the other.

"Sorry that it took so long. They're really busy today," he said as he set the items on the table.

"Why aren't you working if they're this busy?"

Charlie looked around the store as he shrugged out of his coat and hung it on the back of the chair. "I don't know. We've never been quite this busy on Christmas Eve. Allison says they're over staffed too. Somehow I didn't make the cut."

As he took off his scarf and sat down, Sadie studied him.

"Are you upset that they didn't ask you to work?"

Charlie lifted one of the cups from the tray and handed it to her. "I don't think I'm upset. But I'm always one of the first scheduled or called when they think they'll have a rush. I think it's my proximity to the store," he admitted as he took his drink from the tray.

"I guess this was the universe giving you a Christmas gift," Sadie said, smiling at him.

"I suppose it was."

Charlie picked up two napkins, opened them, and set them on the table. He then opened the bag he'd carried to the table and pulled out two muffins. Setting them on the napkins, he then retrieved a plastic knife from the bag and cut one muffin in half.

"Would you like yours cut too?" he asked and Sadie nodded.

"I thought my mother was the only person to do that kind of thing."

Charlie winced. "I learned it from my grandmother, I suppose. Bite-sized everything. Proper manners, and such."

Sadie felt the smile tug at her lips. "I think I appreciate your grandmother."

His eyes lifted. "Would you like to meet her?" he asked, but then his eyes went wide. "Sorry. No, you probably wouldn't like to meet her. That was weird."

"Why was it weird?"

"Because up until today, she hasn't even known who I am. Why take someone new to meet her?"

"Because it's always good to meet new friends," Sadie said, and Charlie's expression softened.

"She says that, you know. I mean she used to."

"Says what?"

Charlie lifted a bite-sized piece of the muffin to his lips. "She used to always say that everyone you meet is a new friend."

"Then I think I would like to meet your grandmother. Even if she never remembers my name or that she met me. At that moment, we could be new friends."

CHAPTER 6

CHARLIE FINALLY TOOK A BITE OF HIS MUFFIN. HE WATCHED AS Sadie pushed up her glasses before she picked up her drink, blew through the small hole in the lid, and then took a sip.

"Do you go to that bookstore often?" he asked.

"All the time. I've been a loyal customer since I was a teenager. Leona is a free spirit, and she makes me feel good."

Charlie assessed how he'd felt when he'd been in the store. Yes, he supposed the woman who owned it had made him feel good too. "So you read a lot?"

Sadie sipped her latte. "I suppose I use books as therapy—or escape," she said, as if that sounded better. "Don't you read?"

"Since I'm working on my master's, I have read quite a bit. But, I can honestly say, none of it is for pleasure." He picked up a piece of his muffin and popped it into his mouth. "Though my grandmother said I should read the book you bought."

"You bought," she reminded him as she lifted her drink to her lips. "You bought both of the books."

"You know what I mean."

"Your grandmother wants you to read it?" Sadie picked up a piece of her muffin and took a delicate bite.

Charlie nodded. "I'm not sure if I have time to read a romance novel."

"It wouldn't take you more than a few hours. I mean, if you're getting a master's degree, I'm sure you read quickly."

He chuckled as he watched her push up her glasses.

"I suppose I do."

Sadie picked up her drink. "Then you should read it. Maybe we could have coffee together again, and you can tell me what you think."

Charlie chewed his lip as he watched her sip her latte. "Okay. I'll read it. But will you still go with me to give my grandmother the other book?"

When she lifted her eyes to meet his, he noticed they were dark with flecks of gold.

"I would love to meet your grandmother," she said as she reached into her bag. "And you can give her the book you bought for her." She pulled the book out and handed it to him.

"Who was Vivian Leigh?" he asked as he looked at the book.

Those dark eyes had gone wide behind her glasses. "You don't know who she was?"

Charlie shook his head. "Should I?"

"Did you ever hear of the movie *Gone With the Wind?*"

"Of course. I've never seen it, but..."

"She played Scarlett O'Hara. It was an epic piece of literature and as epic a movie."

Charlie smiled at her. "Black and white movie?"

"Oh, no. One of the first color movies. Seriously, I can't believe you don't know about it."

Charlie shrugged. "Both of my parents are doctors. And in her prime, my grandmother was an administrator at a hospital too. So I spent a lot of time in daycare and not a lot of time watching TV or movies."

"You come from an impressive lineage." She sipped her latte again. "You said you were getting your master's? In what?"

"Business," he said with a smile, but it ached in his heart. "A master's in business," he repeated.

"Impressive. What kind of business are you in—aside from coffee."

Charlie felt the smile wane. "Not very impressive, is it?"

A line formed between her brows. "What's not?"

"That I work in a coffee shop, and I'll have an MBA."

Sadie leaned in. "Well, don't you have to start somewhere? I mean, I'm sure it's hard to go to school that much and work in corporate America, or build your own business. I'm sure lots of people work in coffee shops while getting their master's."

He nodded slowly. "Yeah, but I would assume some of them know what area they want to be in. I don't."

"You don't know what kind of business to run?"

"I don't even have to run a business. It's a leg up if I have the MBA and a job. It pays better."

She smiled. "Okay, so where do you want a job?"

Charlie lifted his cup to his lips and sipped. "I like it here."

Her eyes moved around the coffee shop. "Here?"

"Yeah. There's something about the same faces every day that come to see you for that moment of familiarity. I know things about people I shouldn't know. I know secrets. I know when something is off, because someone is wearing a green shirt and not a red one. I know how they drink their coffee at six in the morning, and what they drink at three in the afternoon." He let out a breath. "I like it here."

The smile that had formed on her lips widened as she pushed up her glasses again. "So then have an MBA and stay here."

Charlie bit down on his lip. "My parents are doctors. What a disappointment to have a son who only slings coffee."

"I bet they don't really feel that way."

He considered. "I don't know. I've never told them that I'm happy here."

"Maybe it's your calling. You know, there are some very

successful coffee houses that have changed the world." Her brows rose. "Perhaps that's your calling. It feels to me as if it's not the coffee you love. It's the people."

Charlie eased back into his chair. She was right. He loved being surrounded by people every day—different people, and yet the same. It wasn't making a cappuccino at all. It was gathering information while he did it.

"I'm really glad I ran into you, again. Who knew your choice of books would change my life twice."

Sadie laughed as she picked up a bite of her muffin. "I'm glad you feel that way."

Charlie watched as the gold flecks in her eyes shimmered. "What do you do?"

Her smile grew tighter, but eased back to her lips a moment later. "Let's say that I'm in between jobs right at the moment."

CHAPTER 7

MILLIONS OF PEOPLE WERE IN BETWEEN JOBS, SADIE THOUGHT, BUT for some reason, when she said it aloud, it made her cringe.

The thought of starting over in a new job gave her anxiety. She'd thought of asking Leona for a job, but Leona didn't need anyone else in her store. Sadie would just be in the way.

If Sadie were truthful, she'd like to be an author and make a living creating stories for others. But that wasn't something someone did and got a paycheck to live on right away. She knew enough people who had tried their hand at it, and those who made a living at it had already spent years building their brand and writing their books.

"What were you doing before?" Charlie asked as he finished his muffin.

"Bookkeeping. It was for a small company that made boxes. But, after the pandemic, box sales weren't enough to stay open."

His brows drew together. "There are boxes everywhere."

"And there are bigger companies making them."

He nodded slowly. "You know, Isabelle," he turned and pointed to the woman who sat at the register on a stool, "she's going on maternity leave. But I have it under good authority that she's not coming back." He leaned in. "She's going to stay home and raise her baby."

"That makes me very happy," Sadie said, thinking about the missed opportunity her and her mother had to do that, since her father had taken off on them when Sadie was little.

"I can get you a job."

Sadie felt her heart rate kick up. "Oh, I don't…"

"They pay well. I mean, as well as a mom-and-pop coffee shop could. But they do. They take care of their employees, and as you can see, they don't lack for business."

"Do you really think they'd hire me?"

"In a New York minute." Charlie pulled his phone from his pocket, slid his finger over the screen, and then handed it to Sadie. "Put your phone number in here. I'll talk to them on Monday and text you. I mean, ideal for you, you're close to work." He laughed, and she couldn't help but do the same.

Sadie put her information into his phone and handed it back to him.

Then, Charlie lifted his phone to face her. "Say, cheese."

She smiled, but she was sure it was horrible. "I don't think you need to put my face in your phone."

"Why not? It's a great face."

Sadie's mouth dropped open. "Thank you," she stammered out the words as Charlie's eyes lifted from his phone to meet hers.

"It is. You have specks of gold in your eyes that sparkle."

"They're hidden behind these horrible glasses."

Charlie shook his head. "They're not horrible. I think they're great."

Sadie swallowed hard. "Maybe you should be wearing them."

"I had some pretty thick ones in high school. For graduation, my dad gave me vision correction. It was then I realized I had this horrible blond mop on top of my head," he joked as he ran his fingers through his curls.

"I like your hair," Sadie said, lifting her cup to her lips.

Charlie let out a small chuckle as he tucked his phone back in his pocket. "Aren't we a pair?"

"I guess we are."

He leaned in to her. "Let's make a pact. I think you're beautiful, and exciting. And you seem to like my hair," he said, and that made her laugh. "So let's promise one another that we won't speak ill of ourselves, and we'll appreciate that the other one likes those little things we find amiss."

Sadie had to remind herself to breathe. His little monologue had made her heart squeeze, and she was feeling something she'd never—ever—felt before.

Charlie held out his hand to her. "Deal?"

Sadie set her drink on the table, looked at his hand, and shook it. "Deal. It's not going to be easy. I can be easily critical of myself."

"Then part of this deal is to remind the other one that we," he said, motioning between them. "You and I, think the other is perfect."

The smile he wore now showed off a glorious set of white teeth, which Sadie hadn't taken note of until then.

She was smart enough to take everything he was saying with a grain of salt. It was the holiday season after all. People were friendlier and more charming during the holidays.

"Okay," she agreed. "I have to admit, I went to Leona's to pick up a book to make myself feel better this Christmas. Meeting a new friend wasn't expected."

"It's a Christmas bonus," he said, pulling back his hand, picking up his drink, and sipping. "Why did you need something to make you feel better? Is Christmas not your favorite time of the year?"

Sadie kept her smile in place. "Oh, I enjoy it. I love to see people happy. But the holidays at our house were always a bit tough."

He nodded thoughtfully. "Hopefully you'll look at this one as being a memorable one. You know, the year you met a new friend."

Sadie nodded, now feeling that optimism. "I think you're right."

"And, I think my grandma will enjoy you. She loves new friends."

And hadn't he already told her that?

Suddenly, Sadie couldn't wait to meet his grandmother. Though she didn't know too much about Charlie, she could tell he came from good people, even if he didn't know about vintage cinema.

CHAPTER 8

THEY WALKED AMONG THE CROWDS THROUGH THE CENTER OF town. The air had grown colder, and Sadie put her gloved hands in her pockets.

Neither of them, they had learned, owned a car. Luckily, nothing was too far from either of them.

On occasion, Charlie would take the bus to school or to see his grandmother. But he rather enjoyed the task of walking.

Sadie, on the other hand, would Uber to her mother's house a few times a week, on those days her mother couldn't get out of bed to drop by or to pick her up. But she'd kept that part of her story to herself.

As they left the old section of town, the crowds thinned out. The care center was less than a mile away.

Sadie's toes were growing cold, but the walk with her new friend reminded her of the joy of Christmas.

There was just a different feel to everything on Christmas Eve.

"My grandmother's name is Ellen," he said as the care center came into sight.

"That's very informal. Should I call her something else?"

Charlie shook his head. "No. My grandfather died years ago, and everyone calls her Ellen. I call her Grandma Ellen."

"Okay."

"She probably won't remember your name," his voice dipped as he said it.

"I understand. It's okay."

"I think I became too optimistic this morning when she called me by name."

Because she couldn't help it, Sadie reached for his hand. "Deep down, she remembers you. I think that's what this morning meant."

Charlie looked down at their clasped hands, and he squeezed his hand around hers, through the layers of gloves. "Thanks. I needed that."

CHARLIE DIDN'T LET GO OF HER HAND, AND GRATEFULLY, SHE didn't pull her hand back.

He wasn't sure what it was about this woman who loved books, wore lots of layers to keep warm, and wasn't always happy at Christmas. She was easy to talk to, and he found that when she looked at him, his heart raced a little faster.

As they crossed the street to the care center, Charlie finally let go of her hand. "Okay, here we go."

"Are you nervous? Don't you visit her all the time?" Sadie asked as the doors opened, and she pulled off her hat right away.

"I do come all the time. And I know I'm going to leave disappointed. But after this morning, I don't want to leave disappointed again."

"I'll be with you."

Charlie stopped and looked down at her, her glasses fogging over from the change in temperature.

Feeling a lightness in his chest, Charlie lifted his gloved hand to Sadie's cheek. "Thank you."

"Why?"

"I don't know. Being with you just gives me hope."

As they walked down the sterile hallway, nurses and staff members said hello to Charlie. Charlie and Sadie each pulled off articles of outdoor clothing, tucked gloves and hats into pockets, and draped coats over their arms.

By the time they came to a room and stopped, they had both shed the cold outside.

Charlie stood for a moment looking at the door. "This is her room."

"Is she always in there?"

"Usually. Sometimes they take her to the common area. She enjoys that."

Sadie reached for his hand again, and this time they touched, skin to skin. "She'll be happy to see you."

He nodded. "She might not remember my name, but she is always glad to see me."

"That's something."

Charlie looked at her. "You're right, it is."

Keeping his hand in hers, Charlie pushed open the door, and they walked into the room.

The woman who sat in the chair looking out the window looked up at them. Her eyes sparkled, and they were as blue as Charlie's were, Sadie noticed from across the room. Her hair was white, but it was as curly as Charlie's. And her smile was wide, and though not as white as her grandson's, it radiated that happiness she had to see him.

"Hello, Grandma."

Ellen studied him for a long moment, but there wasn't the recollection he'd been hoping for, Sadie knew.

"Tell me your name," she said to him.

Sadie felt him shift, taking in a deep breath. "I'm Charlie. I'm your grandson."

Ellen nodded. "Charlie," she repeated. "My husband is Charlie."

Sadie looked up at him, and the smile he wore was genuine. It might not have been her recognizing him personally, but she knew something. And, obviously, Charlie had been named after his grandfather.

"That's right," he said. "I was named after him. My grandfather."

Ellen nodded again and then turned her attention to Sadie. "Who are you?"

Sadie gave Charlie's hand a squeeze. "My name is Sadie. I'm a friend of your grandson's."

"It's good to have a friend," she said, just as Charlie said she would. "Don't you agree, Charlie?"

He smiled wide, and gave each of them a glance. "It sure is, Grandma."

CHAPTER 9

SADIE PULLED HER HAND FROM CHARLIE'S, AND HE WATCHED AS SHE opened her bag. She pulled out the book he'd bought for his grandmother and handed it to him.

Their eyes met, and she gave him a supportive nod.

Charlie took the book and moved toward his grandmother. "I bought you this book. I know you love your film stars," he said as he knelt down in front of her.

Ellen took the book and studied it. Then she ran her fingers over the cover and smiled. "Vivian Leigh," she said softly and Charlie felt his stomach tighten. Why couldn't she remember him all the time, but she knew those people?

"Yes," he confirmed and exchanged another look with Sadie.

Sadie took a step toward them. "I've read it. It's a wonderful book. I think you'll enjoy it."

His grandmother looked up at her and smiled. "I think I will. What was your name again?"

"Sadie. I'm Charlie's friend."

"Charlie brought me a romance book," she said, as if she didn't realize he was the same one that had brought it. "It was wonderful. You should read it."

"I plan to," Sadie agreed. "I saw a restroom down the hall. I'll be right back," she dismissed herself and Charlie wondered if it was to give him a moment alone with his grandmother.

"SHE'S LOVELY," HIS GRANDMOTHER SAID, PATTING HIS CHEEK.

"I think she is."

"I met your grandfather one day and ran off with him the next," she said clearly, as if they'd been having a normal conversation, and she knew exactly who he was.

Charlie swallowed hard, the emotions stirring inside him threatened to send tears.

His grandmother touched his cheek. "You look just like he did back then."

There was no stopping them now. Charlie batted his eyes to try and control the tears that rolled.

His grandmother's hand remained on his cheek. "My Charlie and I got on a train, and we took it until it stopped. We got married that night." She eased back in her chair. "You know when you love someone. You just know," she said.

Charlie wiped his cheeks. "I've heard you tell that story before, Grandma. I think it's sweet."

"Some things are worth sharing over and over," she said matter-of-factly before picking up the book he'd brought her. "Will you be coming by tomorrow?"

He saw Sadie walk into the room, and he rose to his feet. "I will."

"Tomorrow is Christmas," she told him, and again, he wondered why her mind worked the way it did.

"You're right, Grandma. Tomorrow is Christmas."

His grandmother looked toward the door where Sadie stood. "Read that book, young lady," she said and winked. Charlie hadn't seen her do that in years.

"I will, ma'am."

"Grandma. You call me Grandma."

Now he saw the tears welling in Sadie's eyes. "I will, Grandma."

"That's better. Now you two get. My stories are going to be on TV down the hall. They'll come get me for them."

Charlie leaned in and kissed his grandmother's cheek. "I love you, Grandma."

~

THE AIR NIPPED AT SADIE'S CHEEKS, WHICH WERE DAMP FROM THE tears that she'd shed as she watched Ellen kiss Charlie goodbye.

She turned as Charlie tilted his head back and let out a long, heavy breath that carried on the air. "That was a tad bit emotional," he said, and Sadie adjusted her glasses as they were beginning to fog over from the cold mixed with her hot tears.

"Is she always like that?"

"No. Just today. She remembered me when I came to visit this morning. She eventually remembered me this afternoon." He wiped his eyes and looked at her. "Thank you for coming."

"It was an honor to meet her."

Charlie stepped up toward Sadie, taking her gloved hands in his. "It meant a lot to me. I think it meant a lot to her too."

Sadie smiled up at him. "I'm glad. I don't have any grandmothers, so this was a nice treat."

Charlie moved closer to her. "She's going to be gone soon. I know that."

"But you're making every moment count, aren't you? That means something."

Lifting his gloved hands to her face, Charlie held her gaze. "Do you believe in fate?"

Sadie swallowed hard. "Yes."

"So does my grandmother."

"I could see that."

"I want to kiss you," he said, his face near hers now.

"We just met."

"I don't think we did. Maybe in this life, but..."

Sadie sucked in a breath. "We're emotional."

Charlie nodded, his gloved hands still cupping her cheeks. "Extremely."

The cold swirled around them, and Sadie was sure her common sense had frozen just as her eyelashes had. It was Christmas Eve. Kissing Charlie might be the only gift she'd get.

Lifting her eyes to meet his, she watched as he waited. The apples of his cheeks were red from the cold, but lifted because he was smiling. Those blue eyes were crystal clear as they looked into hers. If she said no, he'd step away. She had no doubt.

But if she gave herself this one little gift, she'd have it forever —in her heart and in her memory anyway.

Sadie lifted her hands to Charlie's chest, and took a step closer to him. Their breath swirled around them. He wasn't going to move in until she gave him permission. He was that kind of gentleman.

"I would like you to kiss me."

He didn't move in right away. The corners of his mouth lifted, and a dimple formed in his cheek. He was gazing at her, and her heart began to race.

"My grandmother said you were lovely."

Now Sadie's lips were trembling. "She did?"

"And then she told me that she'd met my grandfather one day and ran off with him the next. They took a train until it stopped, and they got married."

Sadie bit down on her lip. Now he wasn't making sense.

Charlie smiled again. "This was a good day. Thank you for that."

"All I did was go looking for you."

"Yes, you did," he said as he moved in and pressed his lips to hers.

CHAPTER 10

CHARLIE'S LIPS WERE COLD PRESSED TO HERS, BUT A FIRE BURNED inside of Sadie as they stood there. She hadn't been sure what she'd expected when Charlie said he wanted to kiss her. But as her lips warmed under his, and the kiss lingered, she realized she wanted a kiss that would change her life.

Charlie staggered closer to her, his hands leaving her face and gripping her shoulders. Sadie held tight to the front of his coat with her gloved hands, and their lips softened against one another's as the cold faded away.

Sadie's grip on Charlie's coat released, and her arms lifted around his neck, as Charlie's slipped around her waist.

Now warm, Sadie's lips parted, and they deepened their kiss. How was it possible in her life, she'd never been kissed like this? Had she been waiting her entire life for a man in a bookstore? Was this simply a Christmas dream?

As if they both needed air at the same time, they eased apart. Charlie rested his forehead against hers.

"That was better than I'd expected," he admitted.

"Yeah," Sadie let out a breath. "I've never kissed someone I didn't know," she managed.

Charlie chuckled, but he didn't step away from her. "Our hearts know each other."

Now Sadie stepped back and drew in a breath. "Maybe we should head back into town."

Charlie tucked his hands into his pockets. "I suppose we should."

THEY DIDN'T HAVE MUCH TO SAY NOW, CHARLIE NOTICED AS THEY walked back toward the center of town. The air had grown colder, and as he looked up, he noticed the clouds.

"I think it's going to snow some more," he broke the silence.

"It'll be nice to have a white Christmas."

"It's been a few years." They passed the coffee house, and walked toward the door that would lead up to their apartments. "What are your plans tomorrow?" he asked as Sadie began to search for her keys.

"I guess I'll go to my mother's for lunch. I'll probably make something and take it with me."

"You don't have any plans already? You know, one person brings rolls. Another a main dish. Someone brings a dessert that a cousin once named something else and the name stuck?" he asked with a laugh, then noticed her eyes didn't flash with humor.

Sadie shook her head. "My mother doesn't enjoy Christmas."

"Oh. I guess I never thought that someone wouldn't enjoy Christmas."

"Well, now you know someone." Sadie looked toward the door, but they didn't advance to go in.

Charlie couldn't help but wonder if she was nervous about him following her. Sure, they'd had a nice afternoon, and one heck of a kiss, but was she still sizing him up? What if he were one of those guys who turned on the charm and then attacked her when she got to her apartment?

Well, he wasn't one of those guys. But he supposed she didn't know that.

"Thank you for a lovely day," Charlie said, taking a step back. "I think I'm going to run a few more errands before heading home. Are you free sometime next week? For dinner?"

Sadie pushed up her glasses. "Yes."

"I'll find you. Now that I know you're always nearby," he smiled and waved as he headed back down the street to give her time to settle in without him around.

When he looked back, she was walking through the door. Sixteen steps and she'd be on her landing. Sixteen more, and that was his landing. He just couldn't believe she'd always been that close, and they'd never crossed paths.

Charlie looked at his watch. It was already getting darker, but it wasn't even quite five yet.

The bookstore was usually open late on the weekends, but he wondered how late she would stay open on Christmas Eve. He'd like to get a gift for Sadie. If her mother didn't like Christmas, maybe that meant Sadie didn't get gifts.

The thought terrified him.

Picking up speed in his step, he hurried to the store as a group walked out. So far, the sign was still turned to open.

He pushed open the door, and the woman with all the bracelets stood behind the counter. "Just in time. Last minute gift buying?" she asked.

"Yes." Charlie hurried to the counter. "That woman that I met here yesterday, Sadie, what does she like to read?"

The smile brightened the woman's face. "She reads a little of everything. She is quite fond of romance though."

"Romances, right."

The woman turned and picked up four books sitting on the counter behind her with a sticky note that read Sadie's name. "These were ones that I ordered for the store, but with Sadie in mind. I knew she would love them."

"Does she know they're here?"

The woman shook her head and her butterfly earrings caught the light as they moved. "No. I haven't shown them to her yet. But, if you're looking for books she would be interested in, you might want to give them to her."

Charlie narrowed his gaze on the woman. "You mean you thought that just because I came in and asked about her, or did you have them there for me to buy for her as a gift."

The smile on the woman's lips grew wider as if it were part of her plan. Charlie couldn't help but wonder if maybe the woman had switched the books on purpose as well.

"She loves candles too." She turned and picked up two that were also on the counter. "In the winter she likes the hearty cinnamon ones. But if she's worked up, she lights the peppermint one."

Charlie nodded. "I'll take it all."

The woman began to ring up the sale and then placed each book in a gift bag that already had tissue paper in it. She elegantly wrapped up the candles, so they were protected, and slipped them in the bag.

Charlie pulled his wallet out of his commuter bag and handed her the credit card. The romance novel that he'd bought for Sadie the day before was still in his bag. His grandmother had wanted him to read it. He still wasn't sure about that.

"Her mother doesn't like Christmas," the woman said as she waited for the confirmation of the sale on her screen. "I always make Sadie a nice salve or some lip balm so that she has a gift to open at Christmas."

"She said her mother doesn't like Christmas," Charlie repeated as the woman handed back his credit card. "Why doesn't she like it?"

"That's her story to tell. But if you're going to give her all of this, she'll be very happy. She doesn't get many gifts."

The woman handed him the bag, and he looked at it. The

woman was a genius with wrapping everything in the bag. It was beautiful.

Charlie looked back at the woman. "Did you make her things for Christmas this year?"

She shook her head and steepled her fingers to her chin, which made all the bracelets on her arms clank together. "Oh, no, sweetheart, I gave her something better this year."

"What did you give her?"

"I gave her you."

CHAPTER 11

CHARLIE WASN'T SURE HOW LONG HE HAD STOOD AT THE COUNTER of the bookstore staring at the woman. Eventually, his body took over, and he remembered to breathe and swallow, once he realized he had to close his mouth. Then he blinked.

The woman continued to smile at him. There was no doubt in his mind now that the woman had set him up—them up. She'd switched the books on purpose so that he'd get to know Sadie, and now he was back in her store buying Christmas presents for someone who wouldn't get any otherwise.

"Thank you," he croaked out the words.

"It is my pleasure, Charlie."

He almost asked how she knew his name, but then remembered he'd handed her his credit card.

Trying to remember to put one foot in front of the other, Charlie headed for the door, pushed it open, and as the chimes rang out, he stepped out into the cold air.

There were no more crowds.

The sun had tucked itself away for the evening, and a quick glance at his watch told Charlie it was just after five o'clock. If he hurried to the coffee shop, he could box up some left-over pastries, if there were any left.

When he turned around to look at the bookstore, the lights were off, except for the decorative Christmas lights around the window display. Had the woman been waiting for him to leave?

He continued his walk to the coffee shop. The light behind the counter was the only one on. Allison moved about wiping down counters, so Charlie tapped on the window, and she lifted her head.

Allison held up a finger and smiled wide as she skirted the counter and headed to the door.

"I was hoping you'd stop back by. If you hadn't, I would have come up to your place," she said, stepping back so that Charlie could step inside.

"Why?"

"The owners left you something," she said as she walked back behind the counter and to the back room. A moment later, she came back with an envelope. "Here. We all got one. It's pretty exciting."

Charlie opened the envelope and inside was a stack of twenties. He could only assume there were about two-hundred dollars in the envelope, but he wasn't about to take it out and count it.

"What's this for?"

"We had a good year," Allison squealed. "They're sharing the good fortune. They're also going to throw us a party after the beginning of the year, so we can all celebrate."

"That's fantastic."

"Isn't it?" Allison walked to the back of the store and returned again, this time with her coat and bag. "Oh, and there's a box for you," she said, pointing to the counter as she slipped on her coat. "We divided up all the extras. That's your box."

He enjoyed the people he worked for and with. They'd thought enough of him to make sure he got a box of left over pastries, too.

"Thanks."

"Sure thing." Allison zipped up her coat and pulled her bag over her head so that it draped off of one shoulder and hung in front of her. "How did the rest of your date go?"

Charlie laughed. He hadn't considered it a date, but the kiss at the end sure made it seem like one. "We had a wonderful day."

"Good. She's cute."

"You said that earlier."

"I meant it. She comes in here all the time. Is this where you met her?"

He laughed again. "I didn't meet her until yesterday at the bookstore. I've never seen her here, and she lives just upstairs."

Allison's brows drew together. "You live upstairs."

"I know. How did I miss her all this time?"

The corner of Allison's mouth turned up. "You weren't supposed to meet her until now," she said. "It's fate."

"Ah, that fate word."

"Don't you believe in fate?"

A little too much, he thought. In fact, when he'd brought it up to Sadie, he'd been afraid it had scared her. But the way the day had lined up, how could he not believe in fate?

"I do," he admitted.

"I can't wait to see how this all plays out," Allison said as she pulled her keys from her bag, and they headed toward the door.

Charlie walked through first and waited while Allison pulled the door closed and locked it.

"Thanks for waiting for me and for all this stuff," he said.

"I didn't wait for you, but you're welcome. I hope you have a great Christmas."

Charlie nodded. "I think I will."

Allison waved as she walked away and Charlie looked up at the building. His apartment was on the back side of the building, but Sadie's windows should face the street, he thought.

There was a window with a small glow, perhaps a lamp.

Another apartment was fully lit, as if there was a lot of activity going on inside it. Would she be making dinner in the well-lit apartment? Was she relaxing in the other?

He wondered if she'd be up for some company. He had presents and pastries for her.

No, he didn't want to appear to be stalking her. Then again, he'd gone to the bookstore—he had presents.

Charlie pulled his keys from his pocket and unlocked the door to go upstairs. No, he decided. He wouldn't go knock on her door tonight.

He'd wait until tomorrow.

Tomorrow was Christmas, and from what he'd learned, Sadie could use a little Christmas magic.

Yes, that's what he would do. He'd give her some Christmas magic.

Pulling one of the books and one of the candles from the bag, he climbed the first set of stairs and stood on the second floor. 2B, she'd said, was her apartment. He turned to face that door. Her apartment would have been the one with just the lamp light.

Hopefully she was home.

He set the book and the candle in front of the door, took a deep breath, knocked, and then high tailed it to the stairs so that she didn't see him.

When he was hidden by the wall, he stopped, and listened.

She opened the door, and he could hear the wrapping on the candle and book.

"Hello?" she called out. "Hello? Did someone leave these for me?"

Charlie started up the stairs to his apartment. That would give her a little something to do for the night, he thought.

There was a different beat inside his chest, he thought as he carried the box and the bag of gifts up the last flight of stairs and down the dimly lit hallway toward his apartment.

Then the words that the woman at the bookstore had said danced around in his head as he unlocked his apartment door. *Oh, no, sweetheart, I gave her something better this year. I gave her you.*

CHAPTER 12

SADIE KNEW THAT THE GIFTS HAD COME FROM LEONA'S STORE. She'd recognized the wrapping paper.

With a smile tugging at her cheeks, Sadie set the packages on the table and sat down. Running her fingers over the paper, she felt love swell in her heart. Certainly Leona had sent the gifts, though Sadie was sure Leona hadn't run after knocking, but she might have sent someone.

Usually, Leona made her salves or lip balms. Perhaps she hadn't had time to make any. But a book and one of her favorite candle scents was a perfect alternative.

As she pulled the paper from the book, she smiled down at the illustrated cover art of the romance novel. Then Sadie pulled the paper from the candle. Peppermint.

Picking up the book and the candle, she stood, and walked to her bed. Tossing the book on the bed, she set the candle on the nightstand, and pushed the small Christmas tree back. Opening the drawer of the nightstand, she took out a lighter, lit the candle, and then tucked the lighter back in the drawer and closed it.

In lieu of dinner, Sadie decided on a cup of tea and a bag of microwave popcorn.

She filled the tea kettle, set it on the stove, and turned on the burner. She pulled a bag of popcorn from the cupboard, opened the door to the microwave, and tossed it inside.

As she set the time on the microwave, she thought about the delightful turns the day had taken. Christmas Eve never held surprises for her anymore, but her day had been just that—one surprise after another.

When the kettle whistled and the microwave chimed, Sadie grinned.

She'd started her day only wanting to find Charlie to give him back the book for his grandmother. Hadn't everything changed from that moment she ran into him on the street?

The latte at the coffee shop, meeting his grandmother, and the kiss on the street corner.

Sadie felt her cheeks heat.

The kiss on the street corner.

She blew out a hot breath and felt her grin widen.

It was out of character for her.

Sadie moved the kettle to another burner and the whistle stopped. Then she opened the microwave and pulled out the bag, careful not to burn herself. Pulling down a bowl, she filled it with popcorn, and then popped a piece in her mouth.

Charlie lived upstairs. Or he said he lived upstairs.

She took another piece of popcorn.

Of course, he didn't enter the building when she had. So, was that all a farce?

No, she didn't want to think that it was.

She looked back at her bed where the romance novel sat.

Those books were filled with people who met and fell in love, just as Charlie's grandmother had said she'd done. And wasn't Sadie a sucker for those kinds of books? Didn't she want to believe every word of them?

Sadie took her tea mug from the drying rack at the sink and

filled it with hot water. Then, she pulled out a tea bag from the small canister and dropped it inside.

Though it was dark outside, it was only seven o'clock. Sadie would sit down and read the book, enjoy her dinner, and take in the scent of the candle. Then maybe, just maybe, she'd go upstairs to apartment 3C and see who answered the door.

~

CHARLIE LOOKED AT HIS PHONE AS HE DISCONNECTED THE CALL. His heart rate was at an abnormal level and his skin was clammy

His grandmother had just called him.

On his twentieth birthday she'd called him. That was the last time he'd spoken to his grandmother on the phone.

But she'd called him. She'd called him by name.

He swallowed hard.

Okay, he knew his father was with his grandmother, so he'd probably dialed the phone for her. But had she wanted to call him?

There was no doubt that during that phone call she'd known who he was. She called him by name. She'd mentioned Sadie by name.

Sadie.

Charlie let his head fall back against the cushion of the recliner. What was it about that woman from the bookstore that tied in with his Grandmother?

Oh, no, sweetheart, I gave her something better this year. I gave her you. Leona's words rang in his head again.

Did Leona know his grandmother? Were they in this together? Was he supposed to end up with Sadie? It had to be coincidence, right?

Charlie stood from the chair and walked to his commuter bag. He needed to go down and talk to her.

As he pulled his keys from his bag, the book that his grandmother had given back to him slid out.

Charlie picked it up and looked down at the cover. He'd examined the cover before. The man with the mop of curly blond hair and the woman holding a book.

Charlie set the keys down on the table.

The pull to read the book that had been given to him to give to his grandmother, which then had his grandmother remembering him, was strong.

He looked at the clock on his microwave.

It was only seven o'clock.

The book wasn't too thick. He wasn't a fast reader, but maybe if he sat down and read it, he could get an idea of what had connected with his grandmother.

Were the characters inside just as they were depicted on the cover? Was the man like Charlie, and was the woman lovely, just as his grandmother had said Sadie was?

There was only one way to find out.

Charlie walked to the refrigerator, took out a soda, and walked back to the recliner with the book in his hand.

Setting the soda on the coffee table, Charlie plopped down into the chair that had once sat in his grandparents' house, and opened the book that seemed to have changed many lives in the past day—all because Leona had put it in the wrong bag.

CHAPTER 13

SADIE PRESSED THE BOOK TO HER CHEST AND LET OUT A SIGH. Happily ever after, she thought.

Every book should end with a happily ever after.

The scent of popcorn had faded, and the peppermint candle soothed her as she inhaled deeply.

She was grateful that Leona had dropped the book off for her. It had proved to make Sadie's Christmas Eve delightful.

Sadie crawled off her bed and walked to the window. The streets were bare now, and at that moment, all the lights that illuminated the trees turned off. The air stilled, and Sadie remembered the feeling from childhood—back when Santa visited her a few times.

The air sizzled with a magic she could never find on any other day.

There was magic happening around her. Children were tucked into bed, finding it hard to fall asleep. Parents were rushing about quietly making more magic happen.

A shred of sadness swam in her gut when she realized she hadn't spoken to her mother again that day. Well, Sadie decided, she was just as guilty of not having called her mother as her mother was of not calling her.

Maybe the lack of Christmas magic was all on Sadie. Oh, her mother didn't want any, and her father, well, who knew where he was, but Sadie had long taken solace in knowing there just wasn't any Christmas magic to be had. So, yes, that was on her.

She'd been privy to it all day, she thought as she set the book on the table. Sadie had become as melancholy as her mother over Christmas. She should make it a point to spread Christmas cheer on her own each year.

Heck, next year she was going to have a bigger tree. Who cared that it wouldn't fit well in her tiny apartment? Maybe she'd have a good job next year too. She thought of how the coffee shop had buzzed that morning. Wouldn't that be fun?

Of course, Charlie would be there too, and wasn't that a bonus?

Sadie pressed her fingertips to her lips.

Charlie.

She looked at the time on the microwave clock. It was past ten now, but there was a draw to see him, if he did, in fact, live on the next floor.

Sadie hurried to her bathroom and flicked on the light. There wasn't time to make herself up, and well, would he even know her if she curled her hair or put on makeup?

Picking up the brush, Sadie ran it through her hair and then pulled it into a band, creating a messy bun atop her head.

Pushing up her glasses, she studied herself.

She was pretty, wasn't she? Or as Ellen had put it, *lovely.*

Looking down at her clothes, she realized she'd never changed. She still had on her jeans and the sweatshirt she'd worn that morning—the one she'd bought from Leona's years ago when the last *Harry Potter* book had been released.

What did it matter what she looked like? She was only going to go knock on the door and see if he really lived there, right?

What if he didn't?

Sadie shook her head. No, she was going to do this.

As she walked through her apartment, she pulled one of the origami ornaments off of her little tree. She'd give it to Charlie. After all, one shouldn't knock on someone's door at ten at night without a gift.

CHARLIE RUBBED HIS EYES AND FLIPPED THE PAGE. HE'D NEVER read a romance novel before. The couple happened upon one another, things had gotten in their way, but then the sparks flew. Oh, how they flew.

There had been a few times when Charlie had wiped the bead of sweat from the back of his neck.

Then, there was a mishap—and a misunderstanding. Now he was reading as fast as he could to find out if the couple would reconcile. They needed to reconcile. They loved each other.

Who cared that they had old lovers?

Who cared that one of them thought the other was wrong, they didn't know—right?

He flipped the page and then nearly jumped from his seat when there was a knock at the door.

Charlie looked down at the book.

Wasn't that how the book had started? The man was studying some technical guide when the woman knocked on his door late at night?

Maybe he was making up the sound in his head.

He went back to reading when the knock came again.

No, someone was at *his* door.

Charlie scrambled from his chair, knocking over his soda, and letting out a string of curses.

He picked up the can.

Had he even taken a drink?

Oh, he'd clean it up in a moment.

He hurried to the door and pulled it open, just as he saw someone walking away.

"Hello?" he called after them.

She turned around, and Charlie felt his mouth drop open.

"Hi," she said softly as she walked back toward his apartment. "It's late. I shouldn't have come. I wasn't sure you actually lived here. I thought perhaps that was a pickup line. Actually, I wasn't sure what I thought." She sucked in a breath. "I brought this for you."

She handed him a piece of paper that was folded into a star with crisp edges.

"I have them on my little tree, and on a garland around my apartment. But I thought you'd like one on your tree. Do you have a tree?"

Charlie closed his mouth and watched her as she rambled on.

Sadie pushed up her glasses. "I was reading. I'm always reading," she admitted with a nervous smile. "Someone dropped a book off at my door. It came from Leona, but I don't think she dropped it off. I finished it, and now I'm..." She took a breath. "And now I'm rambling. I should go."

Sadie lifted her hand in a wave and turned around before Charlie reached for her and happened to only grip a piece of her sweatshirt, but it did cause her to turn around.

When she did, her eyes were wide as he stepped to her.

Charlie cupped her face in his hands and stared into those dark eyes, hidden behind those big, beautiful glasses.

Her hands came to his chest, just as they had on the street earlier that day.

Maybe it was the book he was reading—

Maybe it was the magic in the air since it was Christmas Eve—

Maybe it was love he felt pulsing in his chest for the woman, but he had to kiss her.

Throwing caution to the wind, Charlie dipped his head and pressed his lips to hers.

When she pulled him in tighter, he was sure that thing he was feeling was love.

CHAPTER 14

THAT WASN'T WHAT SHE'D EXPECTED TO HAPPEN, SADIE THOUGHT as her eyes closed even tighter and Charlie's arms wrapped around her.

That Christmas magic buzzed around her until she was dizzy.

When Charlie eased back from the kiss, he pressed his forehead to hers. "I didn't expect you."

"I didn't know I was going to come. I guess I wanted to see if you really lived here."

"I do," he said, still holding her tight. "You should come in. Do you have time?"

A giggle escaped her. "I do."

Charlie eased back more and took her hand, then he led her into his apartment.

As he closed the door, Sadie looked around. His apartment was only slightly bigger than hers was. She could see a door to what she assumed was a bedroom, which she didn't have. Otherwise, the layout was the same.

"I have some soda," he offered and then his eyes went wide. "I have to clean up. Don't move."

He hurried to his kitchenette and pulled a towel off the side of the sink. Turning on the faucet, he ran the towel under it, then turned it off and wrung out the towel.

"I kicked over my drink when I went to answer the door," he admitted as she walked back toward the chair and began to clean up the mess.

"I shouldn't have come so late."

"I was up," he quickly said. "I was reading." Charlie pointed to the book that Sadie had originally picked up at Leona's store.

"You were reading the romance I bought? You bought. I mean the book from the store?"

"I was," he nodded as he walked back to the kitchen and rinsed out the towel. "My grandmother wanted me to read it. She called me."

Sadie smiled, and the hint of tears stung her eyes. "She called you?"

Charlie nodded as he draped the towel over the faucet and walked back toward her. "She did. She called me by name and everything." He ran his fingers through is hair and it made the curls pop up. "My dad was with her. He doesn't usually go in to see her. He just checks on her. But he was there. I'm sure he helped her call me."

"That's very sweet."

"Christmas miracle sweet," he said moving closer to her. "Just like bumping into you today."

Sadie lowered her head, diverting her attention, so that she could collect her thoughts. It was then that she noticed the bag by the door. It was a bag from Leona's store, and she could see wrapped books among the paper.

Lifting her eyes back to Charlie, she narrowed her gaze. "Did you leave the book outside my door?"

Charlie's brows shot up. "Yes," he said on a breath.

"Why?"

"For Christmas," he said almost shyly. "I was going to wait until tomorrow, but I thought you could use something for

Christmas Eve. You told me your mother didn't like Christmas, so I thought you'd like a gift."

Those tears that had stung earlier, now began to pool in her eyes. "You went to Leona's store and bought me a book?"

Charlie nodded and then looked at the bag. "I bought you a few. But I was going to save them for Christmas," he defended. "I hope you're not mad."

"Why would I be mad?" The first tear escaped and rolled down her cheek. "I don't get Christmas presents."

Charlie wiped the tear from her cheek with his thumb. "That's what Leona said."

"She told you that?"

"She said she usually gives you salve or lip balm so that you'll have a gift."

Sadie nodded. "She does do that. Usually."

"I think she knew I was going to go into the bookstore to buy you something for Christmas. She'd picked these books for the store with you in mind, and she suggested I get them for you."

Sadie hiccupped a laugh. "That was sweet of her."

He lowered his hand and took hers. "Leona said she didn't make you anything this year."

Sadie shook her head. "She didn't. But that's okay. I don't expect gifts, ever."

"You should. You deserve them."

Her lip trembled now. "Oh, I gave that dream up when I was little. But finding that book at my door was a special surprise. I sat down and read it, and lit the candle."

"She said you like cinnamon in the winter, and peppermint to think by."

Sadie bit down on her bottom lip to keep it still. "I do. I lit the peppermint candle and read the book with a cup of tea and a bag of popcorn."

Charlie's brows drew together again. "Dinner. I never ate dinner."

The absent-mindedness of it made Sadie laugh. "We could have some now."

"It's past ten-thirty. I have pastries from the coffee shop. They saved me some," he offered. "I was going to bring them to your place in the morning, along with your other gifts, so that you could wake up on Christmas morning to something special."

It was then that the rest of the tears broke through and rolled down Sadie's cheeks. She shuddered back a breath and then lifted her glasses to wipe them away.

"I didn't mean to make you sad," Charlie began, and Sadie shook her head.

"No. It's—I mean—I'm not—" She looked up at him, his eyes wide, and she saw it. She knew what he felt inside, and she was sure that the rapid beat of her heart meant the same thing.

Without consent or even thought, Sadie lunged at him, wrapping her arms around his neck. Her mouth covered his, and his arms wrapped around her as they stumbled back, into the coffee table and then onto the couch.

She landed right on top of him, their chins bouncing off one another's.

Sadie looked down at him to make sure he was okay, and she figured he must have been just fine when he reached for the tie in her hair, pulled it out, and then tucked his fingers into her hair.

"It's crazy," he said as he kissed her cheeks, her lips, her nose. "I know that I love you. That's crazy, right? I mean—"

"I love you too," she sucked in a breath. "I don't know how I know, I just know."

They stilled in the heat of the moment and locked eyes. Yeah, she thought, they just knew.

CHAPTER 15

CHARLIE WASN'T SURE WHEN THEY'D FALLEN ASLEEP. HOW COULD they have? They'd been kissing all night long.

One moment he was under her, the next she was under him.

Now, they lay, still dressed and wrapped in a quilt his grandmother had made that hung on the back of his couch.

Sadie stirred in his arms. Her hair covered her face, and when she turned to look up at him, he smiled as she batted away the strands, so she could see.

"Good morning," she yawned and covered her mouth with her hand.

"Good morning. Merry Christmas."

The smile that formed on her lips was wide.

"It is Christmas morning, isn't it?"

"I can give you your presents now," Charlie said as he sat up and untangled himself from her and the quilt.

He stood and walked toward the bag he'd set by the door. As he walked back to the couch, Sadie tucked her hair behind her ears and reached for her glasses, which had ended up on the coffee table at some point.

"You don't have to give me gifts," she said. "I don't have anything for you."

Charlie sat the bag on the coffee table and then sat down next to her. "You're my gift. I know it sounds cheesy, but you are."

Sadie smiled. "Thank you for these."

"Go on. Open them."

Sadie picked up the bag and pulled out the candle. The smile on her mouth grew wider as she sniffed the cinnamon.

She set the candle on the table and picked out one of the books. Just as Leona had said, it was a romance, but Charlie realized he'd never even looked at the books.

"You said Leona had these waiting for me?" she asked.

He nodded. "I asked her what you liked, and she had a pile for you, well, a pile of books she bought for the store with you in mind."

"She does that sometimes." Sadie chuckled as she opened the last book. "*One Night on a Train, the love story of Ellen and Charlie,*" she read the title of the book then handed it to Charlie.

"What?" He took the book and studied it.

The cover wasn't anything special. Illustrated with suitcases and a train. He turned the book over and looked at the back. "The story of two lovers who met by chance and fell in love," he said, and his voice cracked. "They hopped on a train, rode it until it stopped, and got married. The rest is history."

"That's exactly what your grandmother told you."

"I didn't pick this book," he said, looking at it again. "I mean, it was just in the pile."

Sadie laughed again. "I think Leona just knows things."

"She scares me."

Placing her hand over his. "I think your grandmother knows things too."

"Yeah, she knows you're lovely."

When his phone rang, Charlie looked around. He had no idea

where he'd set it, and he was surprised it hadn't died, since he knew it wasn't on the charger.

Fumbling around the chair where he'd been sitting before Sadie arrived, he found it, and quickly swiped his finger over the screen when he saw his father's contact information pop up.

"Dad? What's wrong? Are you okay?" he asked quickly.

"Merry Christmas, son," his father laughed on the other end.

"Merry Christmas."

"Are you okay?"

Charlie looked at Sadie, who was already reading the book. "I'm fine. Just out of sorts."

"Listen, Grandma wants you to go visit her."

"What's wrong with Grandma?" he asked, and that had Sadie's head lifting, her eyes filled with worry.

"Not a thing. In fact, I haven't seen her this spry in a very long time. She wants to see you. She asked for you by name again."

"Wow. That's wonderful."

"And, Charlie, she wants you to bring your girlfriend?" his father phrased it in a question, understandably.

"Right. Okay. We'll be there."

"We'll be there? You do have a girlfriend?"

Charlie reached out his hand to Sadie, who took it. "I do, Dad. I have a girlfriend."

Sadie sat quietly as Charlie finished his phone call. She wasn't sure if the news he'd received was happy or not.

"Everything's okay?" she asked as Charlie disconnected the call and sat looking at the phone.

"Everything's great. My grandmother would like me, *us*," he corrected, "to stop by and visit her."

"She remembers me?"

"She does, I guess. And now I have a few questions for her,"

Charlie said with a chuckle as he reached for the book. "This is coincidence, right?"

Sadie shrugged. "It's sweet, and special, and…"

"The craziest thing that's ever happened to me," he said as he sat down next to Sadie. "I'd never been to that bookstore. I live feet from you, and I've never seen you. My grandmother suddenly knows me. And it's snowing on Christmas."

Sadie turned to look out the window behind her, now illuminated by the sunrise.

"It is snowing."

"When do you have to be at your mom's?"

Sadie's eyes went wide. "I'm not sure. I left my phone at my apartment. If she called, she's probably worried. Well, maybe she's worried."

"Why don't you head back to your place. I'll brush my teeth and change my clothes. Then I'll bring over the pastries. We can have breakfast, and then we'll go see my grandmother."

She nodded. "Okay."

"And then you can go with me to have dinner at my parents' house."

CHAPTER 16

SADIE PUSHED OPEN THE DOOR TO HER APARTMENT, CARRYING THE bag of gifts from Charlie. Her phone sat on the kitchen table, and it rang just as she closed the door behind her.

Setting the bag on the table, she picked up her phone and looked at the ID.

"Hi, Mom. Merry Christmas," she said cheerfully, hoping that it would resonate through to the other end of the call.

"Sadie, are you okay?"

"Yes."

"I called an hour ago and you didn't answer."

Sadie winced. "I was visiting with a neighbor," she said.

"At six in the morning."

Sadie swallowed hard. "Yes. Pastries on Christmas morning."

"That sounds nice. It's snowing."

"I saw that," Sadie said as she sat down in the chair next to her. "What time should we do lunch?"

Her mother let out a sigh. "I don't know, sweetheart. I'm just not feeling my best today."

Sadie rested elbow on the table, and her head in her hand. "Mom, what's wrong?"

69

"I just don't get this holiday. I don't feel it, honey. Maybe you should spend it with your neighbor."

"Don't you want to see me?"

Her mother didn't answer right away. "I see you all the time. How about we have lunch tomorrow. When it's not some frivolous holiday. Really, sweetie, I just want to be alone today."

The very thought broke Sadie's heart. "If that's what you want."

"I think so. You'll be okay, right? I mean, you don't celebrate this silly day either."

Sadie looked at her little tree on the nightstand. "I'll be okay, Mom."

"Good. Let's meet at Pearl's for late breakfast tomorrow at ten."

Batting back tears, Sadie nodded before she spoke. "Okay. I'll see you then. Merry Christmas, Mom."

"Good-bye, honey."

The call disconnected just as the tapping started at the door.

Sadie set her phone down, stood, and pulled open the door.

"Are you okay?" Charlie's smile quickly dissolved when he looked at her.

"My mother doesn't want to see me today. She's not feeling up to it on this frivolous holiday," she said completely before the tears turned into sobs.

Charlie scrambled to step inside the apartment and set the pastry box on the table before pulling Sadie into him.

"It's okay." He kissed the top of her head. "It's what she needs. You have me. I'm here with you. I love you," he whispered in her ear.

"That's as silly as this holiday, right?" Sadie pulled back and wiped her eyes. "I met you yesterday. Now you love me?"

"And you said you loved me too."

She had said that. "I don't know what's real right now."

"We are," he offered taking a step toward her. "C'mon, ten

minutes ago the world was right. Maybe tonight we can take your mom a plate from dinner. You don't have to stay long, and you can just be with her for a moment. I'll go with you."

"How would I explain you?"

His brows drew together, then his face softened. "As your boyfriend, just as I'm going to introduce you to my parents as my girlfriend, because my grandmother already told them you were."

She giggled at that. "Am I?"

"Aren't you?" he asked. "Would you be?"

Sadie closed the distance between them and rested her head to his chest. "I would be."

"Then it's all going to be okay."

∼

AGAIN, CHARLIE AND SADIE WALKED INTO THE CARE FACILITY HAND in hand.

The nurse lifted her head and smiled at Charlie. "Merry Christmas, Charlie. She's in a good mood this morning."

"I was hoping she would be."

"Your dad is still here. He was here last night, and he's here again this morning. She's a miracle, that Ms. Ellen."

Charlie smiled. "She's that."

They walked past the station and toward his grandmother's room, but before they reached the door, Sadie pulled back and Charlie stopped.

She worried her bottom lip. "Your dad is in there?"

"That's what the nurse said. And that's a big deal, trust me."

"Maybe I should wait out—"

Charlie shook his head and stepped to her, his hand still holding hers. "No. Come with me. You were going to meet him tonight anyway. Now's as good a time." Leaning in, he kissed her softly. "Besides, you have that book in your bag I want to ask her about."

"I'm nervous."

"Don't be. You've already met my grandmother, and now you're among family."

Sadie drew in a breath and nodded.

Charlie turned back around and opened the door.

Not only was his father in the room, but so was his mother and his sister. Okay, he thought, Sadie had reason to be nervous now.

As they walked into the room, his father stood from his seat on his grandmother's bed. His grandmother looked up at him with shining eyes and a wide smile.

His mother and sister's expressions hadn't gone unnoticed. Charlie had never been seen holding hands with a woman before. He supposed he'd stunned them all.

"Merry Christmas, Grandma," he said moving in and kissing her cheek, leaving Sadie near the door.

"Merry Christmas, Charlie," she said giving his cheek a pat. Then her eyes moved past him to Sadie. "Sarah? No, Shelly," she tried again. "That's not right either. Sweetheart, tell me your name again."

Charlie watched as Sadie's eyes moved to each person in the room before she landed them on him and his grandmother and smiled.

"It's Sadie, Ellen. My name is Sadie."

"That's right. Come here, Sadie," she said, and cautiously, Sadie moved to her.

His grandmother held out her hands, and Sadie took them. "You read books."

"Yes, ma'am, I do."

"Books are good. Books have wonderful stories in them."

"Yes."

"Some of them are true. Some of them aren't. But they give you hope, don't they?"

Sadie shifted her eyes to Charlie, and he couldn't help but

smile at her. There was something about the book he'd accidentally brought his grandmother that had changed all of their lives.

"Yes, books do give you hope," Sadie agreed.

His grandmother patted Sadie's hand and pulled her in closer. "Some of those stories are true, and history is worth repeating."

CHAPTER 17

THEIR FAMILY VISIT CONTINUED UNTIL CHARLIE'S FATHER GREW
noticeably uncomfortable, which happened when he'd spend too
long at the care center. Though Charlie had thought he would
have wanted to stay longer since Grandma Ellen was doing so
well today. Perhaps his father would come back later—at least
Charlie hoped he would.

As Charlie's family kissed his grandmother goodbye, and so
had Sadie, Charlie moved in to do the same.

His grandmother held tightly to his hand. "Stay with me a
moment longer," she said and Charlie nodded.

He raised his head to look at Sadie. "I'll be out in just a
moment," he said.

Sadie nodded, her coat draped over her arm. She pushed up
her glasses, tucked a loose strand of hair behind her ear, and gave
a small wave to his grandmother before she walked out of the
room.

"She's lovely," his grandmother said as Sadie disappeared.

"She is."

"She's yours."

Charlie smiled. "I just think she might be."

"I have something for you, Charles," she called him for the first time since he was a child. "I need you to fetch it for me."

"Okay," Charlie said, standing erect in front of her. "What do you need."

"In the top drawer of my dresser," she pointed with a shaky finger.

Charlie walked to the dresser and opened the drawer. On one side there was a small box of personal items, and the rest of the drawer was filled with disposable underwear and bras. He swallowed hard.

"On the right-hand side," his grandmother began, "there is a red pouch. It's got a golden cord."

"I found it," Charlie said pulling out the red pouch.

"Bring it to me."

Closing the drawer, Charlie carried the pouch to his grandmother and handed it to her.

Again, with shaky hands, she opened the top of the bag. "Hold out your hands," she instructed.

Charlie knelt down in front of his grandmother and held out his hands, cupped together.

She turned the bag upside down and emptied out the bag.

Three coins, two lapel pins, a brooch, a pair of earrings, and a ring fell into his hands.

His grandmother poked at each piece before pulling the ring from the pile. "Put the rest of the items back in the bag," she said, and Charlie did as he'd been asked. "Now, put that bag back."

Charlie laughed as he stood, walked to the dresser, pulled open the drawer and replaced the bag. When he closed the drawer and turned around, his grandmother was examining the ring.

He walked back toward her and knelt down in front of her again.

"I met your grandfather one day and we took off the next day and got married," she said.

"You told me that," he admitted, thinking of the book Sadie had in her purse that he'd wanted to show his grandmother.

"We took the train until it stopped. We were married sixty years." She turned the ring between her fingers. "He bought me this ring on our five-year anniversary. He'd saved and saved for it."

"It's beautiful."

"Before this we'd used a piece of wire we'd found on the train. I don't even know what the wire went to, but he'd fashioned it into a ring."

"I didn't know that," he said, remembering only the ring she held in her hand.

His grandmother took his hand and pressed the ring into it, folding his fingers over it. "This is for you, Charles, to give to your girl."

"Oh, Grandma, we're not there yet."

"You will be. You love her."

He smiled. "I do."

"I know. She's yours, you know. I saw it the moment she walked in the door."

"Are you sure? I mean, what will everyone else say?"

"I don't care what they say. I'm giving you this ring to give to her. I know what I'm doing."

Charlie nodded. He hoped she'd remember this tomorrow and not think someone had stolen the ring.

"Thank you, Grandma."

"I love you," she said, and Charlie felt as though he may burst into tears. It took everything he had to keep calm in front of her.

"I love you, too."

"Keep reading books, sweet boy. They'll bring you the whole world."

Charlie moved and kissed his grandmother on the cheek. "I'll come back by and see you later tonight."

She shook her head. "Not tonight. We're having pudding tonight. Come tomorrow."

He chuckled. "I'll see you tomorrow then," he agreed as he stood.

Slipping the ring on his pinkie, he picked up his coat and draped it over his arm.

His grandmother had already focused her attention out the window at a bird that had perched on the sill. He'd be back tomorrow, and the day after that. One day she'd call him Charlie or Charles again. And one day she'd just sit quietly, he knew that.

But on that Christmas morning she knew him well enough to give him her wedding ring to give to the woman he loved—the woman he'd just met—just as his grandmother married a man, years ago, that she'd only met.

CHAPTER 18

"Is everything okay?" Charlie's father's voice had him looking up as he walked out of his grandmother's room.

His family stared back at him, and in that mix stood Sadie.

The ring was still clasped in his hand, hidden under his coat.

"Yeah," he said nodding. "Everything is fine. But, can I talk to you for a moment?"

His father's eyes bore into him for a moment before he nodded his acceptance of the talk. Moving to him, his father wrapped his arm around Charlie's shoulders and the two of them walked toward the front door, and then out into the courtyard.

"Your girl is nice," his father said. "I can tell your mom really likes her."

"That's good," Charlie sighed, realizing how cold it was and he was carrying his coat.

"What's on your mind?"

Charlie stopped and looked at his father, then he opened his hand to reveal the ring.

"Why do you have that?" his father asked.

"Grandma Ellen gave it to me."

"Why?"

"To give to Sadie."

His father's brows narrowed. "Is that why she asked me to call you and have you come here?"

Charlie shrugged. "I can only assume so."

"And she didn't think you were just a younger version of my father or something, right?"

Charlie shook his head. "Earlier she mentioned that her husband's name was Charlie, but not that I was him."

"She wants you to give it to Sadie?"

"She keeps telling me that she met grandpa one day and ran off to marry him the next."

The corner of his father's mouth turned up. "She did always tell me that."

"Is it true?"

His father shrugged. "Why wouldn't it be? She told me that story. He told me that story. My grandmother was tight lipped about it," his father chuckled.

"There's a book..."

"About Ellen and Charlie, who run off and get married," his father interrupted him.

"Yes."

"I don't know if it's their story or coincidence—or where she got her story. All I know, is my whole life it's the story she told. It makes her happy to tell it, and she believes in love at first sight. And when you find your true love, you hold on tight and make them yours right away."

Charlie ran his hand over the back of his neck. "I met Sadie on Friday."

His father chewed his bottom lip. "Yet you've already introduced her to your grandmother and got the ring?"

"She gave me the ring."

"I know," he assured him. "But you don't feel what your grandmother assumes you feel?"

Charlie's eyes widened on his father. "No. I do. I mean I know

I love her."

"How do you know?"

Charlie never thought he'd have such a conversation with his father. "When I see her, my mouth goes dry, my heart rate kicks up, I get dizzy," he laughed. "And when I kiss her…"

"I don't want to know."

"Dad, I've never felt like that about anyone."

"I get that way when your mother looks at me. It's been thirty years. I get it."

"What do I do?"

His father shrugged and put his hand on Charlie's shoulder. "I don't have an answer for you. If she's the one, what's the harm in holding on?" his father suggested, but then stepped closer so that he could whisper in his ear. "Then again, what's the harm in grabbing hold now?"

Charlie eased back to study his father, who smiled at him.

"The choice is yours, Charlie. Like I said, your mom really likes her."

His father turned around as Charlie's mother, sister, and Sadie walked out of the care facility.

When Sadie looked up at him, he could see that twinkle from the gold flecks in her eyes, behind her glasses. She was ten feet from him, but he could see that. What did that mean?

He knew the flecks in her eyes, the pitch changes in her voice, rhythm of her heartbeat. He knew the hum she made when he kissed her, and he knew the sound of her breath when she slept.

He'd known her less than forty-eight hours.

Charlie looked back that the care facility where his grandmother lived. He thought of her story, and the book that currently resided in Sadie's purse.

Running his fingers through the mop of curls on his head, he thought about it all. What would it matter if they ran off and got married and then learned about one another? Did anyone really learn everything before they got married?

Then again, why would they have to run off?

And why did they have to hurry? He could ask her. They could live together so they had each other, and they could work at the coffee house together. He'd like to get married before his grandmother passed. He wanted her to see them together, but it didn't have to be tomorrow or the next week.

"Are you okay?" Sadie's soft voice had him blinking hard. He hadn't seen her standing there. "Your family went home. Your dad said he'll come for us before dinner."

Charlie nodded and realized his body shook. Then again, his coat was still draped over his arm.

"I'm fine," he said pulling on his coat, the ring still fisted in his hand. "I have a lot on my mind."

"Do you need some time to…"

"No." He smiled and slipped the ring into the pocket of his coat. "I'm fine. Why don't we go visit your mother?"

Sadie's eyes went wide. "Why?"

"I think she needs some company."

"I thought we were going to do that after dinner."

They had discussed that, he thought. "Let's take her some of the pastries. We still have nearly an entire box."

Sadie nodded. "Okay. But when you meet her, remember how you feel about me right now."

"Why's that?"

"Because I'm not her. It's very important that you remember that."

CHAPTER 19

SADIE SHOULD HAVE TOLD CHARLIE NO TO SEEING HER MOTHER.

They'd gone back to their apartments. Each of them went their separate ways, showered, and changed for Christmas dinner later. They'd collected the box of pastries from the coffee shop that Charlie had, and Sadie put a candle in a gift bag, along with a cookbook she'd had sitting on her shelf for just such an occasion.

"What's the bag for?" Charlie asked, as Sadie shrugged on her coat and tied on her scarf.

"My mother doesn't do Christmas. She doesn't believe in it, and she doesn't enjoy it. However, if I show up on Christmas day without a gift in hand, my day is just a bit harder."

She noticed the line forming between his brows. "I'm sorry I suggested this. Maybe I'm forcing this on you."

Sadie sighed. "You know what, I'm okay with it. I've spent the morning with your grandmother, who should be a crabby old woman, due to her circumstances. But she brings joy to her family."

"She's not always happy like that. Sometimes she doesn't talk at all."

"But I don't think she wants to be like that—unhappy, that is. I know her disease does that to her. My mother chooses not to be happy."

"Why?"

Sadie bit down on her lip. "Because my father didn't love her."

Charlie's mouth made an O shape, but he made no noise.

Sadie shrugged. "Not everyone gets lucky with love. It seems as if your family has done well in that area, but mine didn't."

"Yet, you're willing to love me after just a few days."

"I'm not my mother," she repeated to him, and he nodded. "I don't want what she's settled for. I love sunrises and music. I love pretty things and Christmas lights. I love you."

She saw the color deepen in his cheeks. "We don't have to go to see her if you don't want to."

"I think I do want to. I want her to meet someone who has a full heart."

"Me?"

"Yes."

"She's not going to like me, is she?"

Sadie moved to him, pressing her hands to his chest, she kissed him softly. "She's going to like you just fine. And, it's going to take her a while to find joy in my situation, but she will —eventually."

"My grandma thinks you're lovely," he said again, and it made Sadie laugh.

"That's going to stay with me forever," she admitted.

"I love you." He nipped her nose with a kiss. "I'm very grateful that woman mixed up our books."

Sadie snorted out a laugh. Yeah, she was very sure Leona hadn't done that by accident.

∼

CHARLIE WAS SURPRISED THAT THEY WERE ABLE TO GET AN UBER, but the driver said he was Jewish, and it was his pleasure to drive everyone around to their celebrations on Christmas.

"I get to meet so many people who are in joyous moods," the driver said as he drove away from their apartments. "My family and I will serve dinner at the shelter later too. You have to give back, right?"

Charlie nodded. He thought the day had been filled with positivity, and he wondered what was in store for them when they arrived at Sadie's mother's house.

He tucked his hand into his pocket and felt for the ring. It was still there, right where he needed it.

Sadie's thumbs were flying over her phone screen, and then she tucked her phone back into her purse.

"Well, she knows we're coming," she said.

"And what did she say?"

The smile on her lips was tight. "That she has to clean the house and get ready. That I should just go back home, she's not ready for company. That she has a bottle of wine she could open. That she's excited to meet you. That she can't believe I could find a man. That she wants to go back to bed. That she's happy you're coming to meet her."

Charlie blinked hard. "She said all of that in that text?"

Sadie nodded. "Yep."

He took her hand and interlaced their fingers. "It's going to be fine. Today seems to be filled with all of those Christmas miracles."

"I didn't tell her I met you on Friday."

"I understand."

"I'm worried that she'll be very nice to you, but have nothing nice to say after."

"I understand that too."

Sadie pressed her hand to her stomach. "I wasn't this nervous meeting your grandmother."

Charlie pressed a kiss to her temple. "It's going to be okay."

~

CHARLIE TIPPED THE DRIVER TWENTY DOLLARS. HE FIGURED SINCE the owners of the coffee shop had been so generous with their bonus, he could be generous too.

Sadie stood looking up at the brownstone. Charlie noticed it was the only one in the row without some kind of holiday decor.

When the door opened, he had to wonder if they'd arrived at the right house.

The woman standing at the top of the steps had dark hair, like Sadie's, but it was curled and flowed to her shoulders. She was in a dress that was tied at the waist and skimmed her knees. She had on makeup, and Charlie could see her red nail polish from the street. This didn't look like a woman who was spending the day in bed.

"Merry Christmas, Mom," Sadie said as she began to walk up the steps.

"Merry Christmas, honey." Her mother reached for her as they neared the door. Pulling her in, she kissed Sadie's cheeks, and Charlie could see the lipstick marks it left when she turned around to him.

"Mom, this is Charlie."

Her mother reached out her hand to him. "I'm Trudy."

Charlie shook her hand, his still gloved. "It's a pleasure to meet you."

"Come in. Come in," she offered, and they both stepped inside.

The wood was dark, and the rooms were dark. Okay, maybe she'd been shut inside for a while. He could smell candles burning, and a tea kettle began to whistle.

"I thought we'd have some tea. C'mon back," Trudy said as she hurried to the back of the house.

Sadie began to take off her coat and hang it on the rack by the door. "The adventure begins," she said as she started toward the kitchen, and Charlie followed.

CHAPTER 20

Trudy poured hot water into three antique teacups, which were plated on saucers. Sadie pulled down small plates and napkins for the pastries, and Charlie watched as they worked around one another, as if anticipating one to say something, but neither did.

Trudy carried over a small box filled with tea bags to the table and set them in front of him.

"It was nice of you to bring pastries. I go into that coffee shop when I'm on that side of town. I don't remember seeing you there," she said as she went back for the teacups.

"Oh, I'm around. I'm in graduate school as well, so sometimes I work odd hours. Sadie had never seen me there either," he admitted, and Sadie smiled at him.

Trudy shifted a look between them. "Then how did you meet?"

Sadie walked to the table with the plates. "Leona."

"Ohhh," her mother drew out the word. "How is Leona?"

"She's wonderful. The store has been very busy."

"Hmmm," her mother again drew out the sound. "Well, that's

nice. I'm surprised I haven't met you yet, Charles. Or heard much about you."

And there they had it, he thought. This was where things would go south. He'd seen Sadie flinch, so he reached for her hand and covered it with hers to let her know he'd take the lead.

"There isn't much to tell about me. I work. I go to school. I'm in town quite a bit, so I don't have a car to get out this way. But Sadie and I both have a love of coffee and books. Actually, my grandmother has a love of books. I was buying her books when I met Sadie."

She gave him a grateful look.

"You were buying your grandmother books?" Trudy carried two cups to the table, and Sadie went for the last one.

"I was. She's in a care facility, but she has a thing for old movie stars. I'd bought her a book on Vivian Leigh. But, funny story, when I gave her the book, it was a different book. The woman at the store got them mixed up. She'd given me Sadie's book, and her the one on Vivian Leigh. But my grandmother loved it. She hadn't called me by name in a long time, but she did after she read it."

Trudy sat down next to him and picked a tea bag, which she ripped into. "That's quite a story."

"Oh, she's quite a woman," he kept talking and he noticed the slightest curl on Sadie's lips as she sat quietly. "She's had dementia for a bit. She humors us when we visit, on days she doesn't know us. She never makes us feel as if we're strangers who have come to hurt her. But, she's quiet. Then there are days, like when I took her the book and she'd read it, and she remembered me, she talked to Sadie, and my dad, who doesn't like to sit there and only checks in on her, had been visiting too. She even called for me to come back to see her. It's been remarkable."

Trudy looked at Sadie. "You've met his grandmother?"

Sadie bit down on a pastry and nodded. "I have. I wanted to make sure she got the right book."

Trudy scowled but then turned her attention back to Charlie. "It all sounds very sweet." She pursed her lips. "Did Sadie tell you she's currently unemployed?"

Charlie noticed Sadie's reaction to her mother's malicious remark, and he hurried to talk again. "She did. We talked about getting her a job at the coffee shop too. It's so close to where she lives, and the people that own it are extremely caring. We have a woman going on maternity leave next week, and we all know she's not coming back. It's a great opportunity for Sadie to start there."

He knew she was grateful for him jumping in. He wasn't sure he could keep talking like he was, though. He was wearing out. Charlie had to assume this was why Sadie would get worked up when she mentioned her mother.

"That sounds nice," Trudy pushed her teacup away. "I hadn't expected to see you today," her mother said with barely a glance out of the side of her eye.

"Charlie wanted to meet you," Sadie said sweetly.

He took a bite from his pastry. "I did. She said you didn't have plans. So, I appreciate you letting us visit."

Trudy's shoulders softened. "It's been nice."

THEY'D VISITED FOR AN HOUR BEFORE TRUDY BEGAN TAPPING HER fingers on the table, and Charlie knew that was a tell for her. He'd wanted to show her the ring he was going to give to Sadie, but over the course of that hour, he'd defused more potential bombs than he could have imagined.

No, he didn't see Sadie in her mother at all, and he felt for Trudy. It had to be miserable to be so lonely and so angry at the only person who truly loved her.

Trudy had excused herself to lay down, and Sadie cleaned up the kitchen. Charlie helped her dry the cups, and they left the pastry box on the table.

"Thank you," Sadie whispered.

"You don't have to thank me."

"You kept her calm."

"I've had practice with my grandmother, I guess. All I did was keep talking."

She leaned into him as she turned off the water at the sink. "I love you."

"I love you too. And for the record, I know you're nothing alike."

CHAPTER 21

CHARLIE HAD CALLED FOR ANOTHER UBER TO TAKE THEM TO HIS parents' house. He thought after the visit with her mother, Sadie could use a good dose of family.

Her mother hadn't even thanked her for the gift she'd brought, though she had, just as Sadie had said, seemed to expect it.

Sadie's head rested on his shoulder as they drove through town.

"Do you still have that book in your purse?" Charlie asked.

"Yes," Sadie said, sitting up and opening her purse. She pulled the book out and handed it to him. "We forgot to ask your grandmother about it."

Charlie flipped through the pages. "I wonder if my grandmother knows the woman at the bookstore. Or if she did once."

"Do you think that's why Leona gave you that book to give to me?"

Charlie shrugged. "There's a lot of coincidences, isn't there?"

She rested her head back to his shoulder. "I suppose, but I don't care. I don't remember a Christmas where I was happy. And I'm happy."

Charlie looked at the book. He didn't know the name of the author. And, heck any good romance would have a quick love trope and a happily ever after, right? He flipped through the book. The table of contents had the chapters listed and each one had a title. There was one entitled *The Proposal.*

He turned to the page.

I thought he had lost his mind. We'd taken a walk, hand in hand, in the setting sun. Somehow we'd ended at the train station, and we sat, holding hands, on one of the benches outside the depot.

Charlie skimmed over a few more pages before reading again.

"Well?" he said, and I realized my mouth had gone dry.

"I don't think I heard you right. What did you say?"

Charlie chuckled. "I asked you if you'd marry me."

Suddenly, I couldn't breathe. I hadn't known him but a few hours, but in my heart, I've known him my entire life. Why did I know that there was nothing I wanted more than to marry this man I'd only just met?

"Well?" he asked again.

"Oh—oh, boy," I said, holding my hand over my heart. "That would be crazy, wouldn't it?"

"Of course it would be. But what an adventure, right? I mean, really, how long do you have to know someone before you know it's right? I knew I loved you the moment I saw you. It was solidified the moment I heard your voice. And, Ellen, I know we will have a long and happy life together."

"But we don't know anything about each other."

"Right. What a wonderful opportunity to learn." He adjusted in his seat. "Think about it. Some people court for years. Do they really know each other better than we know each other? Let's buy train tickets and take the train until it stops. Then let's get married wherever it stops."

I swallowed hard and bit my lip. What would my mother say? What would my father say?

And in that very moment, I knew I didn't care.

Charlie was right. I knew I loved him, and I'd have my entire life to learn about him.

"Okay," I said. "I will marry you."

"You will?"

"I will."

He pulled me to him and kissed me hard on the mouth. "I love you, Ellen. This will be a story to tell our grandkids about, won't it?"

Charlie closed the book and let out a breath—*their grandchildren.*

"Are you okay?" Sadie sat up and looked at him. Again, those flecks of gold in her eyes flashed at him.

"Yeah. You know what, I am okay."

Charlie adjusted in the backseat of the Honda that had picked them up. The book rested on his lap, and he stuck his hand into his coat pocket.

"My grandparents met and got married. My grandfather figured they'd have their whole life to learn about one another."

Sadie laughed. "That's true."

He pulled out the ring and held it in his hand. Sadie's eyes went wide, and she sucked in a breath.

"My grandmother wanted me to visit her today so she could give me this."

Sadie licked her lips. "What is that?"

"It's her wedding ring. Not her original, which was a piece of wire, but the one my grandfather replaced it with."

"Oh."

"She thinks you're lovely."

Sadie let out a little laugh. "You've said that."

"Right." Charlie looked at the ring in his hand. "She wanted me to give this to you."

"Why? She just met me."

Charlie lifted his eyes to meet hers. "Why?" He let out a little chuckle. "She wants me to marry you."

"Oh," Sadie said again before she tucked her lips between her teeth.

"I'm doing this all wrong." Charlie noticed the woman driving the car looking at him in the review mirror. God, he should have waited. How horrible was this proposal?

Sadie covered his hand with hers. "No. You're doing it all right."

There was a change in the air, and he knew she felt it. Maybe she created it.

"I want to marry you, Sadie. I want what they had. I want to tell my grandkids this story."

Tears pooled in her eyes and spilled over to her cheeks. "I want to tell them this story too. I want to tell this story to your grandmother."

Charlie chuckled. "Right. She'll like it, even if she doesn't know us." He held the ring between his fingers, and with his other hand, he took Sadie's hand. "Will you marry me? A stranger you met at a bookstore only two days ago?"

Sadie's lips trembled, but it was the driver's sobs that caught both of their attention.

"Don't mind me," the woman said as she wiped away tears.

Sadie laughed as she looked down at their hands and then back up to him. "I will marry you. And I will share this story with our grandchildren—and I hope they find love, too. The kind of love we're going to share for the rest of our lives."

Charlie slid the ring on her finger. "Merry Christmas, Sadie— my wife-to-be."

Cupping his face, Sadie pulled him in to kiss him. "Merry Christmas, Charlie. I know you're going to be the most amazing husband ever."

PART II
IN WITH THE OLD

CHAPTER 22

LEONA WATCHED SADIE HANG HEARTS IN THE FRONT WINDOW OF the store for their Valentine's display. Why she hadn't hired the woman years ago, she wasn't sure. Perhaps she'd been afraid of losing one of her best customers.

As Sadie fastened a heart, the light coming through the window caught the ring on her finger and Leona smiled. She knew that if she mixed up those books that day, true love would find her sweet Sadie, and it had. Now Sadie was engaged to Charlie, and they were getting married that summer. They'd recently moved into his grandmother's house, and Leona thought that had made their love story go full circle.

When the chimes rang above the door, Leona watched as a woman walked into the store and her attention went straight to Sadie hanging decorations in the window.

"That's looking lovely," the woman said, and Sadie looked down at her from her perch on the ladder.

"Thank you," Sadie replied.

The woman continued to look around the store, though she hadn't stepped in more than a foot. "Can I help you find anything?" Leona asked.

Walking toward the counter, the woman held out her hand. "I'm Fiona Gable. I'm an author."

When they heard Sadie gasp, both women looked at her as she scurried down the ladder.

"You're Fiona Gable?" Sadie asked, her eyes wide.

"Yes."

"You wrote the book about Charlie and Ellen," she said, then scurried behind the counter, pulled out her bag, and retrieved the book from inside.

Fiona's eyes went wide, and she pulled back her hand, which Leona had yet to shake. "Yes, I did." There was an uneasy smile on the woman's mouth, and Leona watched as Sadie set the book on the counter.

"How do you know them?"

"Know who?" Fiona asked.

"Charlie and Ellen."

Fiona exchanged glances with Leona before looking back at Sadie. "I don't know them. I made them up."

Sadie shook her head. "No. Ellen and Charlie are real." She held out her hand. "Charlie McGowan is my fiancé. The young Charlie McGowan," she said with a laugh. "His grandfather was also Charlie McGowan and his grandmother is Ellen. They met one night, got on a train, and got married where it stopped. This is their story."

A line deepened between Fiona's brows. "I'm so sorry to disappoint you. I don't know them, or their story—personally that is."

Sadie's shoulders dropped. "That's too bad. His grandmother has dementia, but she can still tell this story." Sadie looked down at the book. "Maybe she read it and thinks it's her story."

Fiona chewed her bottom lip. "I would be honored to sign your copy though."

Sadie smiled. "I would like that."

Sadie pushed the book across the counter, and retrieved a pen from the cup next to the register.

"What was your name?" Fiona asked.

"I'm Sadie, but actually, will you sign it to Ellen? I think I'll give her the book."

FIONA TURNED THE BOOK TOWARD HERSELF, THE PEN SHAKING between her fingers. The story was hers. She'd created it. She'd written it.

Well, she'd heard the story from her ex-husband, and she'd embellished it.

Never had she thought it was more than a tall tale that someone had passed down. God, she'd heard more than one story like that.

Fiona opened the book to the title page and signed the book as she had thousands before. She kept it basic with Ellen's name and her professional signature, because she didn't know what she'd say.

Sliding the book back to Sadie, she smiled. "I hope she'll enjoy the story."

Sadie took the book, held it to her chest. "It's a wonderful story. My fiancé and I got engaged within three days. We're getting married this summer. But it was his grandmother who encouraged us."

"That's a very sweet story."

The older of the women who had been behind the counter smiled at her. "It's an honor to have you in our little store."

"It's a stunning store. I've just relocated to the area, and I always have to check out the local bookstores."

The woman held her hand out to Fiona, again. "I'm Leona. The *Happily Ever After Bookstore* is my gem."

"And it is a gem," Fiona agreed.

"We carry some of your books. Perhaps we could schedule a book signing."

Fiona hadn't come to the store hoping to book a signing, but the thought thrilled her. "I would love that. I do have a new book coming out in a few weeks."

"*Light and Bright*," Leona said. "Our shipment arrives next week. If you're not otherwise committed, we could do a release party. I'll order more books."

"That's not much time to plan."

"Oh, we have a very loyal clientele. We'll fill the store."

Fiona placed her hand over her heart. "I would really appreciate that." She felt the tears sting, and she cleared her throat. "I'm sorry. The past few years have been a little emotional for me. It'll be nice to celebrate again."

"We're happy we can help." Leona pushed a notepad toward her. "Why don't you leave me your phone number and your email address. We'll put everything together."

Fiona wrote down her phone number and email address. "I do appreciate it."

"It's our pleasure."

Fiona let out a breath. "Well, I think I'll continue strolling through town. It's awfully cute. I thought I saw a coffee shop."

Sadie's eyes lit. "My fiancé works there. He's there now. Charlie. You can't miss him. He's the one with blond, curly hair."

Fiona nodded. "I'll look for him. Thank you both again," she said as she hiked her purse up on her shoulder. "I look forward to hearing from you."

Fiona turned to walk out of the store, but she stopped when she saw the small bulletin board on the wall by the door.

There were business cards for salons, lawn services, and pet sitting. But in the center of the board was a flyer for the Richter Rock Quartet, and smiling from the center of the photo was the man who broke her heart into a million pieces for his own dream.

She looked at the dates, the flyer was old.

Drawing in a breath and letting it out slowly, she let herself out of the bookstore. It was best that their paths didn't cross. Fiona wasn't sure she could handle it.

CHAPTER 23

Fiona had met Charlie at the coffee shop, though she was sure the entire staff wanted to have her removed from the store.

She'd ordered her drink and moved down the line. The man behind the counter began to concoct the drink, as per her instructions written on the side of the cup, but when he looked up and smiled at her, she felt as if she'd been socked in the gut.

His eyes, the curve of his face, the dimple in his cheek, and the hair—the hair!

Charlie McGowan stood before her just as she'd written him in her book. She stared, for a long moment when he'd asked her how she was doing.

Fiona's mouth had gone dry and fallen open. Her eyes locked on him, and the woman working next to him inched in closer as if to protect Charlie from the crazy woman at the counter.

"Ma'am, are you okay?" the woman asked, and Fiona choked on her breath.

"I'm fine. I'm fine." She smiled as Charlie went back to work on her drink. "Are you the Charlie who is engaged to the woman at the bookstore?"

He lifted those familiar eyes to meet hers again. "Yes, ma'am." A smile curled up the corner of his mouth. "That's my girl."

"She's charming. She sent me down here."

The woman next to Charlie elbowed him sweetly as he handed off the coffee cup, and she filled the top with whipped cream. "She's our best salesperson," he laughed. "She sends lots of business our way."

"Well, it was a pleasure to meet you," Fiona said, moving down the line as Charlie picked up the next cup to create another drink.

"Have a great day, Ms. Fiona." Charlie said back, obviously remembering her name that was written on the cup.

Collecting her drink at the end of the counter, Fiona noticed the flyer on the bulletin board next to the door at the coffee shop too.

Suddenly, the past hour had exhausted her, and the thought that she might be done exploring for the day crossed her mind. It was time to go home and write down her feelings.

～

THE COLD MADE PRICE'S HAND, ARM, AND SHOULDER ACHE IN THE brace they'd given him after the van accident. He'd heard people talk about their joints aching when the weather changed, and now he had to assume he'd be part of that group of people.

Well, he wasn't thirty years old anymore, heck he wasn't forty, or even fifty. On that last birthday, he'd turned fifty-five—the day they'd left town and the van skidded on an icy corner, flipped and ended the tour for the Richter Rock Quartet.

This new town had become home to him—at least until Phil, the drummer who had been driving the van—woke up from his coma. When everyone was healed, and home, then Price would leave. Until then, he'd recover there too.

With his arm held gingerly in front of him, in the sling that kept his limb still, Price walked down the quaint street that ran through the center of town. He wasn't in the mood for coffee, though he'd frequented the store in the week that he'd been there. The antique shop had a few items he'd love to take home with him, but he'd refrained. As he continued his walk, he stopped outside the bookstore. He hadn't managed to go inside yet, and why would he?

The woman standing in the front window on the ladder hanging up shiny hearts caught his eye. She pushed up her glasses, looked at her work, and then noticed him watching her. He waved, and then so did she with a smile.

It was then he noticed the book in the corner of the window and sighed. Yep, that's why he hadn't gone into the store. He hadn't wanted to see the name Fiona Gable—but there it was.

Oh, heck, he couldn't play music. He couldn't write music either with his arm like it was. He might as well go inside and buy a book to keep him company. There were hundreds of authors represented in the store, he didn't have to buy a book with the name of the woman he'd walked away from—the woman that he loved.

Price backtracked a few steps and pushed open the door to the store. A chime rang out above him. Again, the woman on the ladder looked at him and smiled. Another woman wrapped a gift at the counter for a customer.

"Hi," the woman behind the counter greeted. "Let me know if I can help you find anything."

"Thanks," Price said as he wandered further into the store.

He appreciated the eclectic mix of books. There were used books and new books. Candles adorned one shelf, and charms, crystals, and rocks on the other

With his back purposely turned away from the romance section, he studied the biographies. He did like to learn about other people.

"Are you finding what you came for?"

Price's head shot up, and the woman who had been standing behind the counter was now standing next to him. Looking at her, he would have thought he'd have heard her walking toward him with all those bracelets on her arm.

"Just thought I'd pick up a book. I'm stuck in town for a bit. A book would keep me company."

The woman smiled, a stack of books in her arms. "Books are great friends," she said. "I was just shelving these. You like biographies?"

Price nodded with a shrug, which sent a pain through his arm.

The woman juggled the stack in her hands. "I have a new Abe Lincoln biography, and let's see," she said, moving to another book. "Here's one about Neil Armstrong."

Price watched her restack the books in her arms. "The one with the orange cover. What was the title on that?"

She shifted the stack again. "*A Winter in Connecticut.*"

Without having been asked, the woman handed Price the book, and he felt the heat transfer from the book through his skin.

Instinctively, he turned the book over and looked at the back. There she was. Fiona Gable with her bright smile, twinkling eyes, and hair, which he'd watched turn to silver throughout the time they'd spent together.

"She'll be here signing books," the woman told him. "She has a new book coming out. Have you read her?"

Price attempted to keep his smile from taking over. "Oh, yes. I've read them all," he said. He just didn't mention that he'd read most of them as stacks of paper on the kitchen table.

"Then I hope to see you come for the signing." She studied him for a moment. "You look awfully familiar. You've been in the store before?"

Price shook his head. "My photo is on your bulletin board for the quartet."

She let out a hum. "You performed last week."

"We did."

"Rock quartet? What is that exactly?"

Price grinned. He was used to that question and had often thought they should change the name of the group. But they'd worked hard to create their own style, and it worked.

"We started out as a classical quartet, and then we added some rock to our style. That came about when drummer, an old hippy, joined."

"Oh," the woman nodded, and he had to assume she hadn't heard their music, or she'd have understood. "You're still in town?"

Price held the book in one hand and nodded to the one in the brace. "Our van had an accident. I'm sticking around town until all the members of my quartet and our crew are okay. Our drummer is bad off."

The woman rested her hand on his good arm. "I'm sorry to hear that. Let him know that we wish him a speedy recovery," she said, and Price hoped he got one. "We buy back books too if you're looking to fill time with books." She winked. "You could go to the library, too, but our shelves are more current," she smiled, then walked down another aisle with the stack of books in her arm.

CHAPTER 24

Fiona braced herself against the cold February morning. She'd gone to the coffee shop, and was surprised to find that Charlie's fiancée worked there too.

She'd reminded Fiona that her name was Sadie, which was a good thing, because in the mindset that Fiona was in, she'd have called her Ellen.

In the week that she'd been in town, she'd made a point to go to the coffee shop every day. There was a pull to see Charlie in the flesh. Of course, she understood that her character and that man had nothing in common, really. It was a coincidence. Besides, the Charlie that she'd concocted would have been nearly one-hundred years old by now. But seeing that mop of blond curls and those piercing blue eyes every morning seemed to bring Fiona some peace. Especially, since every store in town still had that flyer up with her ex-husband's face on it. Seriously, how was she supposed to make a new start when he peered at her from every doorway? And why didn't they all update those bulletin boards?

Now, with coffee in hand, she headed toward the bookstore.

Pushing open the door, then turning to make sure it closed

quickly as to not let in the cold, she looked around. It was eerily quiet.

Fiona pulled her phone from her pocket. It was only eight o'clock in the morning.

Leona stepped out of the back room, a cup in her hand with a tea strainer dangling from her fingers.

"Good morning," she said cheerfully, as if Fiona hadn't just barged in before she opened her store.

"I just realized what time it was. I'm so sorry to just bust in like this. You're not even open yet. I didn't even look for lights on or the open sign," which she turned to see was set to CLOSED.

"It's a brisk morning for a walk," Leona said as she perched herself on a stool behind the counter, still unfazed by Fiona. "I have another stool," she offered as she set her tea up on the counter, hopped off her stool, and pulled up another next to her. "Sit for a bit."

Fiona bit down on her lip and it stung. She needed to get some lip balm. She'd buy some from the bookstore, she decided. It was the least she could do for intruding early.

"Thank you," Fiona said as she sat down, still bundled in her coat and scarf.

"We received our books for your signing. And the extra shipment will arrive right before. I've already pre-sold most of my first shipment. I think we'll have a nice crowd."

Fiona swallowed hard. "You've sold that many books?"

"I told you, we have a loyal clientele."

"I'd say so." She sipped her coffee and winced. She'd forgotten it wasn't just a regular coffee, but a mix of creams and flavors she just wasn't prepared for. "I was hoping I could do some research this morning. All of my copies of my books are in storage. Everything won't fit in my new place." She lifted her hand to her hair to push it back, only to find a pencil tucked into the wiry curls she'd forgotten to tame.

Pulling the pencil from her hair, she tucked it into her coat pocket.

"Anyway, this past week I've been cranking out a new book. It seems as if I have a lot of feelings about this town."

"Inspirational?"

Fiona winced. "You could say that, I suppose." She sipped her coffee again, this time prepared for what she'd taste. "I swear, I didn't know Charlie and Ellen McGowan."

Leona smiled. "With Mrs. McGowan's state of mind, it's easy for her to assume that the book was about her."

"A little too coincidental though, don't you think?"

Leona shrugged. "I've learned that the world works in amazing ways," she said with a wink. "Besides, if you spend time in my store, you walk away with a happily ever after. That's my motto."

Fiona wondered exactly what that was supposed to mean as she sipped her coffee again. Fiona wasn't feeling happily ever after at the moment. Not with having met the McGowans, or future McGowans, and having Price's face in every doorway.

She let out a steady breath. No, for the first time, she was writing something that might not have a happy ending. Then again, maybe it would never see the light of day, and it was all for therapy. After all, she was relocating to find herself.

"You said you came to do some research?" Leona reminded her.

"Yes," Fiona said, setting her coffee on the counter and pulling a slip of paper from her pocket. "I often go back through my books and find things I've written so that I don't repeat myself, or I can expand on something. I just wanted to go through a few of my books and look for certain passages. I'm happy to use the used section, as to not mar any new copies."

"You don't have them on your computer?"

Fiona felt that crack in her lip again as she bit down. "They're on a hard drive—in storage," she said, knowing full well that hard drive she was thinking of had nearly thirty years of memories from her marriage to Price on it too. If she were to find her new self, she had to tuck away the old one.

"You have free rein," Leona offered with a smile. "But beware, if I get busy, I might put you to work."

"I don't think that seems so horrible."

"Sadie hung around too long." Leona laughed. "You see that I've put her to work too."

"She's a sweet girl."

"She is. And she got her happily ever after in this store too," Leona said, smiling as she looked up at the clock.

Fiona watched as Leona stood, walked to the door and turned the sign around, and then turned on the lights. As she slipped back behind the counter, she picked up an iPod, which must have been an original, and scrolled through the selection.

Fiona watched as the door opened and, as if the entire town knew that Leona had just turned the sign, customers began to walk through the door.

Then, she heard the music Leona had started as a customer approached the counter and engaged Leona in conversation.

The Richter Rock Quartet played quietly through the speakers. Fiona closed her eyes tightly as she lifted her cup to her lips. *Fiona's Wedding March*, played to the patrons in the store, who couldn't even hear it, but to Fiona, it shook her to her core.

Price had written it for her so many years ago. It had become the first song that they'd recorded and had been played on the radio. Fiona's hands trembled now, as she remembered dancing in the rain as they heard it play.

That was a lifetime ago, she thought. This was now.

CHAPTER 25

THE BOOKSTORE HAD BEEN BUZZING SINCE FIONA HAD WALKED IN at three-thirty the afternoon of her signing. She'd been in daily since she'd been doing research, and she'd watched Leona and Sadie decorate in anticipation. However, she couldn't have imagined that when she walked through the door, the line would be stretched outside and down the block.

The people in line knew who she was as she hurried past them. She'd heard the whispers and then there was applause. The smile tugging at her cheeks nearly hurt as she said hello to everyone and hurried inside.

"Good afternoon," Leona met her and enveloped her in a hug. "I think your fans are eager to meet you."

"I do have the time right, right?"

"You do. They've been lined up for two hours. The coffee shop even donated coffee to the people outside in the cold."

"I don't know what to say. This is so much more than I'd expected."

Leona smiled wide as she began to help Fiona out of her coat. "Go in the back and help yourself to some coffee or tea and a snack. Start time is four o'clock."

Fiona nodded as Leona took her coat and placed it on the rack behind the counter.

In the small back room, Fiona found a small coffee pot balanced on a shelf. The pot still steamed.

She took one of the foam cups and filled it with coffee, then added the lid. Realizing her hands shook, because she'd been so nervous she'd forgotten to eat, she took a muffin from the tray, next to the coffee pot, and bit into it.

Fiona had had book signings before—even ones with long lines. But it had been years. Books had been released, but she hadn't even been sure they were any good. *A Winter in Connecticut* had been her last bestseller, and often she thought the end of her happiness.

Light and Bright had been her trying to find happiness in the romances that she wrote. She'd written it in less than a month, locked in her apartment in New York, hidden away from the world. She'd poured every last ounce of what she'd remembered about love into that book. Now, she felt hollow and the stuff she was writing proved it.

Her agent wasn't going to like it. It was dark and sad. There was no romance, how could there be? The only man she'd ever loved—the one who made it so that she could write romances—had chosen his career over her almost a decade ago.

Fiona took another bite of her muffin. Now, older and wiser, Fiona knew that she'd carried that baggage in her heart for too long. In the past decade, she'd learned a lot and had grown as a person. So, her books would be different now. She was different now. A woman in her fifties didn't see life the same as a woman in her thirties or forties. And Fiona wasn't the only woman in the world. No, she'd be appreciated for her raw take on life. Maybe romance was dead.

The door to the back room opened, and a smiling Sadie looked at her. "I wanted to see if you needed anything."

Fiona chewed her last bite. "I'm just fueling up."

"Good. I've never seen a line this long."

"I don't understand it either. I'm not a hot commodity anymore."

Sadie laughed. "I think you are. Let me know if you need anything. I've been working the line. We will sell all your books today. Some people have requested other books, and we're ringing them right up while they wait."

Fiona drew in a breath. "I can't thank you and Leona enough for what you've done. I had no idea something like this would happen in my life when I pulled up to this town."

"It's Leona. I swear she has some kind of magic over people when it comes to books."

Sadie stepped back through the door and let it close.

Fiona considered what she'd said, and she had to agree. Leona and her little bookstore were magical.

PRICE LOOKED AT THE LINE OUTSIDE THE BOOKSTORE. THEN, HE looked down at the book in his hand. *A Winter in Connecticut.* He'd put in an order for Fiona's newest release, which he'd claim when he made it through the door.

Pride swelled in his chest seeing so many people gather to celebrate Fiona.

He looked at his watch. The time for her signing was coming to an end, but the line was still out the door. A man walked up beside him, and Price recognized the man carrying trays of coffee.

"Would you like a coffee?" the man asked.

"That's generous of you," Price said, tucking the book against him, using his braced arm, and took a cup with his good hand.

"Well, we figure you all need something warm since you're standing out in the cold."

"You look familiar. I mean, I know I've probably seen you at the coffee shop."

"My fiancée works in the bookstore."

"No, there's something else. What's your name?"

"Charlie," the man said, looking down at his trays as if he thought he should shake Price's hand, but realized his hands were full. "Charlie McGowan."

Price knew his eyes went wide. He swallowed hard. "No kidding?" he asked and cleared his throat.

"I know, Ms. Gable wrote a book, coincidentally with my name."

"Coincidentally, huh?"

"That's what I've heard, though the story is one my grandmother always told me about her and my grandfather."

Price swallowed hard again. "Your grandfather was Charlie too?"

"Yes, sir."

"And I assume your grandmother is Ellen?"

Charlie nodded. "You've read the book?"

Of course he had. Hadn't he been the one to tell her the story, which landed her the agent, who got her the contract, and the rest was history?

"Yes, I've read it."

CHAPTER 26

PRICE WAITED HIS TURN, EVENTUALLY MAKING IT INSIDE, INTO THE warmth of the store. He could see her now.

Fiona sat at a table, the young woman—the future Mrs. McGowan—standing next to the table helping facilitate the many people handing Fiona books to sign.

The woman behind him tapped him on the shoulder to have him move forward when he realized he'd just been staring at Fiona.

It had been eight years since he'd been near her, and suddenly it ached in his heart.

Her hair was shorter than she used to wear it, and peppered with silver. Price smiled. She was never one to cover up those little bits of aging, and he admired that. The closer he got, he could see that with age had brought a softness to her body, and that too he appreciated. Once an athlete, he knew that the destruction of their marriage had put her into a depression, and she'd stopped running. But looking at her, he thought the softness only added to her appeal.

Price looked down at the book in the crook of his arm. *A Winter in Connecticut* had precisely depicted what she went through when he'd chosen his career over marriage and trying to have more children—or their undesirable lack of children, as the case was. He winced. That hadn't been her fault, her body just couldn't carry a child to term, but somewhere, he was sure he'd made it her fault.

The woman who owned the store, Leona, he remembered, moved in next to him.

"Here's your copy of her new book. I read it this morning. It— it's…" she let out a sigh, "breathtaking."

"She doesn't disappoint," he said and his voice hitched.

"Will she be okay seeing you?" Leona asked in a whisper and Price narrowed his eyes.

"I hope she will be. I assume you've done some deep digging into her?"

Leona rested her hand on his arm. "I read people. I know when she walks into the store, she takes a moment with your photo on the bulletin board."

"That show was weeks ago," he reminded Leona, finding it humorous that all the stores still had the flyer hanging up.

"There's an unspoken rule that you must keep those things up," she laughed and then looked behind him. "There are only ten more people after you. Why don't you go to the end of the line. It'll give you a few moments to talk to her then."

Price looked behind him. The woman was either being very courteous to her customers, or hoping to avoid a scene if Fiona didn't react to him well.

He nodded in acceptance and stepped out of line. Leona walked him to the back of the line and then put a sandwich board behind him that said that the signing was over.

"You have these kinds of events a lot?" he asked, noting the printed sign.

"All the time. And much like Ms. Gable's, sometimes the line never stops. She's already over her promised time. But she said she didn't mind."

"I'm sure she doesn't. She'd never turn away someone who wanted to meet her and discuss her stories."

Leona folded her arms. "She's created quite a stir here with her books. Especially for Charlie and Sadie," she mentioned the name of the fiancée of the man at the coffee shop. "She's been coming in and doing research through her old books, and using the table in the corner to write. I think she's got something new brewing. I'm excited to see what it is."

"She's been here?"

Leona nodded. "She lives in town now. Starting over in a new place."

The woman at the front of the line took Leona's attention away from him, and he watched as Leona greeted everyone in line as she moved toward the front.

As the line moved him toward the table where his ex-wife sat, an enormous smile permeated her lips, and he realized his palms had grown damp.

So, they were in the same town now. Though, he didn't know how long he'd be there. Some of the members of his band, and their team, had gone home. But some remained in the hospital, and he wouldn't leave them.

The woman in front of him gave her name to Sadie, who wrote it on a sticky note and placed it inside the book right where Fiona would sign. It was a good method to make sure the name was spelled right and easily found on the right page to save time. Hadn't he once done that for her when she'd written that first book? Pride still swelled in him when he thought of it.

As he approached, Sadie turned to speak to someone who had walked up behind her. It was now his turn, and there would be no sticky note, no open to the right page.

Price swallowed hard as Fiona turned her head to take a sip from a bottle of water she kept at her side, on the ground, away from the books.

He set both books on the table, and her well-manicured hand came to the first one and pulled it toward her.

"Who should I make this out to?" she asked, obviously aware that Sadie hadn't helped, and it was the end of the line. Her eyes hadn't yet lifted as she picked up her pen.

"Price," he said, and then her head lifted, and her bright blue eyes went wide.

CHAPTER 27

"OH. OH—HI," FIONA STAMMERED AS PRICE SMILED DOWN AT HER. "Why are you here? You stood in line? You're here?" her voice cracked as she looked over him, her eyes landing on his arm. "What happened to you? You're here?"

It seemed as if everyone in the store had disappeared. It was only them.

"I came in the other day, and they said you'd be here signing. I couldn't pass up the opportunity to see you. How are you, Fi?"

Fi. He was the only person to ever call her that, and it shouldn't have twisted inside her as it had.

Fiona gave it some thought. How was she?

"I'm fine," she said, her pen still between her fingers hovering over the page of the book.

"You look good," he said, and his mouth curled into that smile that had sold her on the young musician when she too was younger.

"Thank you. Did you really come to have me sign these for you?" She looked down at the book on the table.

"Of course I did. I have every book you've ever published, and a few that you didn't," he confessed, and she remembered having written him a few books that were for his eyes only.

She looked up at him, taking in the full sight of him.

His hair was mostly white now, and lines had creased around his eyes. The beard wasn't new. He'd toyed with one on and off for years, but now it was speckled with the same white that filled his hair.

Fiona looked down, again, at the book she was poised to sign. Flipping the book closed, she read the title. *A Winter in Connecticut*. It had been her healer, she thought of it—the book she wrote after they'd parted.

"I remember it being a much better winter than that," Price said, causing her to lift her eyes to him again.

"This is fiction."

"Is it?"

Fiona bit down on her lip. "What happened to you?" she asked him, again, looking at his arm.

Price looked down at the brace that held his arm in place. "We performed here a few weeks ago."

"I know. No one removes their flyers."

He chuckled. "We got into an accident outside of town. Phil was driving the van. We hit some ice and the van flipped."

Fiona gasped, holding her hands to her chest. "That's horrible. You got hurt? Who else got hurt?"

"Everyone," he said, chuckling, but she knew it was out of pain. "Phil is in a coma. The other guys have some broken bones, and all. I dislocated my shoulder and sprained my wrist. A few more weeks in this thing."

Now Fiona rose to her feet and moved around the table. "Phil is really bad then?"

"Severe head trauma. I'm staying here until everyone is healed and home."

"That could be a long time."

"As long as it takes, Fi." He was gazing into her eyes. "You're beautiful."

Fiona swallowed hard. "Thank you." She looked around the store which was now sans people. Somehow, she'd signed up until close.

Leona and Sadie sat behind the counter closing out the register.

Price looked around as well. "Looks like you closed down the store."

"I guess I did."

"I met Charlie McGowan today. Well, the younger one," he said, and Fiona flinched.

"You owe me an explanation."

"Over dinner?" Price asked.

Fiona walked back around the table, sat down, and picked up her pen. "I don't suppose that's a good idea."

"Why not?"

"We're divorced," she reminded him as she began to sign his books.

"Divorced people can eat together, you know."

She finished writing and closed the books. Handing them back to him, she kept her eyes on him. "Okay. Since you're in town and so am I."

"I hear you live here now."

"It was time for change."

"Interesting that you landed here." He tucked the books in the crook of his injured arm. "Seven o'clock at Miner's?"

"Okay," she agreed.

Price smiled at her. "It was really nice to see you. I'll see you at dinner."

Fiona watched Price turn to leave the store. As he passed by the counter, he said his goodbyes to Leona and Sadie as well. Then, both women turned their attention to her.

Her wonderful day had taken an awkward turn.

It had only taken a moment for Leona and Sadie to walk over to her, both grinning like teenage girls.

"What a way to finish your day, huh?" Sadie asked. "Price Richter came to have you sign books for him?"

Both Fiona and Leona shifted a glance at the younger woman.

"What? He didn't come to meet you?"

Leona laughed first, and Fiona felt it wash over her until she laughed too.

"Oh, my sweet Sadie. Price is my ex-husband."

Sadie's eyes went wide. "Oh. Oh! I didn't know that." She looked at Leona. "You knew that? How did you know that?"

Leona shrugged and then adjusted the many bracelets on her arm. "She looks at the flyer each day that she walks in. It was a guess that there was something, so I googled it."

Fiona shook her head. "He asked me to dinner."

Leona reached a hand to Fiona's arm. "Are you going?"

"I am. I haven't talked to him in nearly eight years, but we were married for decades."

Sadie shifted a glance between them. "Won't it be awkward? I mean you're divorced."

"But we can be civil. We split amicably."

"If it was amicable, why split?"

Fiona realized just how young their dear Sadie must be. "Sometimes your heart loves a person, but your calling takes you in a different direction. That's what happened to us." Fiona drew in a deep breath because Sadie's statement now resonated differently in her chest. "Of course, I haven't talked to him in years. Maybe it will be awkward. Certainly we aren't the same people we were when we parted ways."

"I think you'll be just fine. The hard part is over. He talked to you." Leona said, grinning. "He's in town for a while."

"He mentioned the accident. My heart breaks for Phil, their drummer."

"I heard he was in a coma from one of our customers," Leona confirmed.

Fiona nodded and then let out a long breath. "Well, I must say this was one of my most successful book signings. You sure did make my release day something special. I absolutely appreciate everything you've done for me."

"It's our pleasure," Leona said. "You'll be back tomorrow to research and write?"

"I suppose I will be."

"Good. Then you can fill us in on your date."

CHAPTER 28

FIONA WALKED TOWARD MINER'S JUST BEFORE SEVEN O'CLOCK. HER toes and nose were cold, and her hands shook—though that could have been from the cold, but it was most likely her nerves.

She could have driven, or taken a ride, but she'd chosen to walk to clear her head. Now, standing outside the restaurant, with its warm glow spilling out onto the street, she reconsidered the entire invitation.

Wasn't the reason she'd never talked to Price after their divorce was because she was a sucker for him? He could easily have pulled her along on a string and kept her as one of his girls in the city.

She shook away the thought. Oh, she'd accused him of that enough, but even she didn't believe that while they were married he had women in each town. He could have, but she didn't think he did.

It was one dinner. One night. One more memory to write in a book of fiction, that depicted her life in some way.

"You could have waited inside for me," Price's voice came from behind her, and she turned.

"I was just taking a moment," Fiona confessed.

"Nervous?"

Fiona gripped her purse to her as if it were a safety harness. "It's been a long time since I've sat down and talked to you —civilly."

Price smiled. "I have no doubt that once we warm up, we'll be comfortable around each other again." He gestured to the door. "I made reservations."

Fiona turned and pulled open the door and Price caught it with his foot. She hadn't considered even maneuvering through doors would be hard with one arm, since the other was in a sling.

He moved to the counter and gave his name. The young woman nodded, but didn't give him any recognition. Fiona supposed that a rock quartet wasn't famous among twenty-somethings. And, since there hadn't been a movie with their songs on a soundtrack for years, perhaps he and his band had faded into the backdrop of society now. His flyers on bulletin boards would confirm that, she thought again.

Wouldn't that be a change for him, she wondered.

They followed the woman to a small corner booth in the back of the restaurant. Fiona was sure he'd requested it. It was how he worked. She didn't assume he'd asked to hide them in the dark corner in order to make moves on her. His request for secluded tables came from a time when his music was chosen by millions of brides as their wedding song, followed by a sweet love song he'd written for her for her birthday. Women had once swooned over the man, whose hand was at the small of her back. They'd thrown themselves at him, even with obedient men standing by their sides. It was no wonder she'd accused him so many times of infidelity.

One flash of that smile had her knees go weak, and she knew just how romantic and sensitive a lover he was. She couldn't fault any woman for wanting to find out for themselves.

Fiona shrugged out of her coat, tucking it into the corner of the booth before she scooted in.

Then she watched as Price did the same, though with more difficulty.

She should have offered to help him, but the thought hadn't even crossed her mind until she watched him struggle with grace. Hadn't he always had a grace about him? It was part of his charm, and what made him easy to be around.

Carefully, he slid into the booth across from her.

"You don't look comfortable. We could ask them to move us to a table," she offered.

"I'll be just fine. It doesn't matter where I sit, until this is gone, comfort isn't part of my day to day."

Fiona let her shoulders fall. "My heart hurts for Phil and his family."

"Rosalyn flew in to be with him. She's been by his side since they got him stabilized."

"They're still married?" Fiona asked.

Price's brows rose. "No. Divorce ran through the quartet and the crew like a virus for about a decade. But, Rosalyn still loves the man, and he loves her."

"So why divorce?" she asked, then felt the vile taste of her words. Hadn't Sadie asked her the same thing?

"In their case, someone else got in the way," Price offered, as he picked up the glass of water that was on the table and sipped.

"Phil had a girl in each town?" Fiona bit the inside of her cheek after she'd said it. God, she couldn't be civil around him.

"No, it so happened that she had a co-worker that she'd gotten very cozy with. His wife found out and let Phil in on it."

Fiona winced. "That's horrible."

"That's life," he said nonchalantly. "It was ugly. It was dirty. And he still loves Rosalyn, and it's evident she loves him too. Sometimes tragedy brings people around."

Fiona's stomach tightened. "Will you keep playing?"

Price shrugged his unconfined shoulder. "This might have been a sign. It doesn't mean I stop writing, or recording. Seriously, there haven't been any good wedding songs for years," he humored.

The server approached the table, and Fiona was grateful for the moment to collect herself.

Price ordered a bottle of wine and the server retreated.

"I assume you still drink wine," he said as an afterthought.

"Not often. But yes."

He nodded slowly, and she knew he was letting the words 'not often' resonate. Wine had been her escape, perhaps her demon, in the last years of their marriage. And until that very moment, she hadn't even considered that it might have been the reason for the demise of their love affair.

Picking up her water glass, Fiona steadied it with both hands and sipped from it.

That was a lot to process, she thought.

She made a mental note to herself to look into *A Winter in Connecticut* tomorrow. Perhaps she'd written about it there, in the pages of someone else's story. Maybe she'd find the answers to what she was feeling sitting across from the only man she'd ever loved.

CHAPTER 29

THEY WERE SILENT AS THEY STUDIED THE MENUS. PRICE HAD EATEN there many times in the past week, but now he seemed to not know what was on the menu. Maybe he just couldn't concentrate having Fi so close to him.

He'd dreamed of this moment, he thought. In his notebook of lyric ideas, he'd written this—the moment they could be together again and just be civil.

It had been a long decade without her, and the past eight, when they hadn't spoken, had been lonely.

Above all, Fi had always been his friend. Perhaps he'd missed that most.

When the server returned, Price put down his menu.

Fiona looked up at the woman. "I'll have the penne and a salad, dressing on the side, please."

Price felt the corner of his mouth turn up with a smile. Always on the side, he mused.

"I'll have chicken piccata and my salad fully dressed," he added and noted that Fiona's lips curled into a smile, just as his had when she'd ordered.

When the server walked away, Fiona lifted her glass of wine. "Some things never change, huh?"

"Comforting thought, really." He lifted his glass and held it out toward her. "Here's to your new release. May it be a great success."

Fiona tapped her glass to his. "Thank you."

"I'll post my review tomorrow," he offered as he sipped his wine.

Fiona's brows rose. "You'll go back and read it tonight?"

"Of course. I always read your books on the day they release."

She worried her lip and set the glass down on the table. "Price, maybe don't read this one."

Her hesitation humored him, and he eased back against the booth, and then adjusted the sling on his arm. "You did me no favors in the Connecticut book. I can't imagine you can rip me apart any more almost a decade later."

Fiona batted her eyes, and he noticed they'd gone damp. "I'm so sorry."

"Why? Because we divorced and you healed through your writing? Obviously, you don't listen to my music anymore."

"I try not to."

Price sipped his wine again. "Creatives will use that channel to get over their pain. We two creatives, just happen to be known by the public. Personal feelings then become public ones."

"It's all fictional," she confirmed as she sipped her wine.

"The names have been changed to protect the innocent. I can read between the lines."

Again, she tugged her lip between her teeth. "I didn't mean to hurt you."

"Sure you did. *Farewell to You*, maybe don't listen to that song," he teased and Fiona actually laughed.

"Speaking of changing names to protect the innocent—" she lifted her glass. "Charlie and Ellen McGowan?"

Price pushed his glass back, but kept his fingers around the base of the glass stem. "Who knew that'd come around, huh?"

Without drinking, Fiona set her glass back on the table. "I look stupid. You told me that story."

"I did."

"That woman thinks that's her story. Her grandson thinks it's her story."

"It is."

Fiona's eyes went wide, and she leaned over the table on her arms. "I shouldn't have written it then."

"It got you a contract."

"It's stealing someone's story."

"It's a beautiful love story."

"You're an idiot."

"You could come up with a much more poetic way to tell me that. I've read your books, remember."

The color in her cheeks grew darker, and this was how he knew how to handle her, he thought. Though, it wasn't what he'd wanted when he invited her to dinner.

"Fi, I'm sorry."

"Sorry. You know they could have sued me. They still could. God, Price, I've met Charlie McGowan. Well, the younger Charlie McGowan." She pushed back her hair, which she always did in frustration. "I have to be able to tell them something about the book."

"Tell them the truth. I told you the story, and you wrote it."

"They could come after you."

"They could. They won't. It's a beautiful story."

"Why did you give me those names? Heck, I could have changed them, but you insisted."

Price nodded. "It's their story."

Fiona blew out a breath. "And where did you hear that story?"

"From Charlie McGowan himself," Price admitted. "The old Charlie McGowan."

Fiona pressed her fingers to her temples. "When did you meet him?"

"Right before I met you." He smiled. "I think his story was still in my heart."

Price readjusted himself for comfort and sipped his wine.

Collecting his thoughts, he took in a breath. "Let's see, he was probably in his sixties or early seventies then. I have no idea. Snow white hair and lines of a life well lived on his face. I met him on a train, and that was part of what started the conversation about him and his wife. They'd been married for forty years then, and he was a smitten man."

Price chuckled when he recalled how the man's eyes sparkled as he'd told him the story.

"Fi, I wanted what he had. I remember thinking, when I feel like I did when he told me that story, I'd know I found the woman of my dreams." He lifted his eyes to meet hers. "When I met you, that's how I felt."

Her hand shook as she reached for her wine and took a long sip, and then another. "You asked me to marry you two days after we met."

The smile on his mouth was genuine. "I did."

"Because of Charlie?"

"I didn't want to miss my opportunity."

"I was twenty."

He shrugged. "Love knows no age. And, if I remember correctly, you told me yes."

Fiona pushed away her glass. "I did."

"And three years later, you finally married me," he teased, and now she laughed. "And I still felt the way I did after hearing Charlie's story."

Fiona wrapped her arms around herself, and eased back into the booth. "We had some good years."

"A lot of them," he reminded her.

"We had a lot of loss too."

Price's heart ached in his chest now. "Yes, we did."

"You should have left after the first loss."

"Fi, are you kidding me?"

A tear fell from her eye and streaked down her cheek. "You deserved a family."

"You are my family."

"Was."

"Are," he protested.

Needing to be near her now, he managed out of his side of the booth, aware of how awkward he must have looked. Standing, he walked to her side and slid in next to her.

"There was never a time you didn't know how much I wanted a child," he said. "But you can't still put all the blame on yourself."

"Sure I can," she said, wiping tears from her cheeks. "I lost them. Me. My body. Six babies, Price. Six."

"And now we have six angels waiting for us in heaven." He brushed his hand over her hair, and then his thumb over her wet cheek. "We weren't meant to be parents on earth."

Her lips trembled, and he wanted to kiss them, but he refrained. His words had already caused her too much pain.

CHAPTER 30

Fiona walked into the bookstore and Leona took one look at her and hurried toward her.

Again, she realized she was earlier than opening, but her mind was still in a haze.

"You don't look well," Leona said as she moved to her. "Maybe you should sit down."

Fiona blinked hard. "I came to work on my book. I need to work."

"C'mon, let's get you some tea."

With Leona's arm wrapped around her shoulders, Fiona leaned into her as they walked to the back room. When they'd entered the small space, Leona lowered Fiona into a chair and went about making a cup of tea.

"I can't decide if your date went well, or not," Leona said. "You either look as if you're angry, or you took him home and didn't get any sleep."

Again, Fiona blinked hard, then she laughed. "His arm is in a sling. I don't think taking him home and—well, whatever—was an option."

"I don't think that would have stopped him. But, okay, I don't think you did that."

"I didn't."

Leona set a cup in front of Fiona, a tea bag bobbing around inside. "Thank you."

Leona gave her a nod, pulled up the stepstool next to Fiona, and sat down. "You fought?"

Fiona wrapped her hands around the mug. "Argued. Poked. Reminisced. Accused. Laughed. Mourned."

Crossing her legs and wrapping her hands around her knees, Leona leaned in. "That's a lot for one dinner."

"Half a dinner. Once it was brought to the table, we boxed it up and decided to call it a night."

"And he went home with you?"

Fiona shook her head. "No. It was all either of us could handle. Twenty plus years of marriage, and we can't even sit for one entire meal."

Leona reached for Fiona's hands. "I think it was only a start. I've read your books. You still love him."

"I write fiction."

"Okay, if you say so," Leona humored. "*A Winter in Connecticut* was when you broke up. *Light and Bright* is you trying to move on. But, you haven't moved on, have you?"

Fiona didn't like the comparison, but wasn't that true enough? Her books were a scrapbook of her life—only changed for the better. "Sure I have. I live here now."

"And he's here."

"For the moment."

Leona shrugged. "So he says. I heard through the grapevine that Phil woke up."

Tears pooled in Fiona's eyes. "I'm so happy to hear that."

"I still don't think Price will leave."

"Why would he stay?"

Leona patted Fiona's hands. "Because you're here." She stood.

"Happily ever afters are cultivated here, remember? I know you understand happily ever afters. I've read all your books."

Fiona let the breath that had caught in her lungs sit there as she watched Leona walk out to the store and close the door behind her.

When she felt her head go light, Fiona let out the breath she held.

She and Price didn't have a happily ever after. If they had, wouldn't one of those six angels have been left for them?

Fiona clasped her hands together as they'd began to shake.

Things would make sense again once Price left town. Now that Phil was awake, it was only a matter of time. She could wait it out.

~

PRICE SAT AT HIS FRIEND'S BEDSIDE AS A NURSE TENDED TO HIM. His own arm was aching in the sling that confined it.

When the nurse left, Phil let out a breath.

"I'm sorry, man. I'm so sorry," Phil nearly wept.

"Not one bit of that was your fault. It happens."

"I could have killed someone. Look at you."

"I'm fine. Everyone is fine. And now you're awake and healing."

Phil closed his eyes. "My head hurts all the time."

"I can't imagine that'll go away anytime soon. But I will be here until they let you go. And, I have a small place if we need to stay longer."

Phil opened his eyes. "Where are we anyway?"

That caused Price to laugh. "Were in a town where fate brought us."

Phil winced as he slightly turned his head toward Price. "Fate brought us here and caused this?"

"Fi lives here now," Price said, and he couldn't help but smile.

"And you knew that?"

"I don't think she lived here until after we played here. I don't know. But I've seen her. I've talked to her. I had dinner with her."

"You fought, and now you're here with me. Same story."

The realism of that socked Price in the gut. "I don't want it to be the same story. She keeps writing happily ever after endings to our love story, so I have to believe she thinks about it."

"You're old now," Phil coughed.

"I'm ten years younger than you, old man."

A smile curled on Phil's dry lips. "Roslyn has been here, hasn't she?"

"The whole time."

"Love is blind, man. Why would she do that?"

"For the same reason you're smiling about it," Price said. "Because she loves you."

"She'll get over it."

"I don't think so, or she wouldn't have come."

Price watched as Phil adjusted himself in the bed. "And it's the same reason you're going to live here now too, huh? With or without me?" Phil coughed again, and Price was sure that the accident was the end of the man's smoking, or so he hoped.

"Do you think that's what I'm going to do?"

"You've never loved anyone but Fiona. Hell, you always have two or three ratted books of hers in your possession to read, or look at her photo on the back. You chose your career, but you didn't really."

Price should have known the man knew him that well. Who else knew those things, he wondered.

"She's aged," Price smiled. "She's gained twenty pounds, her eyes are creased, her hair is speckled with gray."

"And your eyes just lit up because you still think she's the most beautiful woman you've ever seen in your life."

Now Price's smile was wide, and it tugged at his cheeks. "I

can't help it. I knew the minute I met her I wanted her in my life. All these years later, I still feel it."

"Then why are you here? Go get her."

Price's smile faded and guilt weighed heavy on his chest. "She's still devastated about all the miscarriages."

"Oh, man."

"That's a lot of loss for a woman to carry."

"You carried it too. Maybe you need to remind her of that. Yeah, you are probably not going to get another chance where kids are concerned, but you had the love of a good woman." Phil chuckled again. "Heck, so did I."

"You still do."

Price watched as Phil ran his tongue over his teeth. "We're both stupid men."

"No one would ever argue that."

"Let's make a pact," Phil said, moving, and then wincing. "We get 'em back."

"Who? Our wives?"

"Yep. Our gig is up and we know it. It's time to settle down for good, pal. And you deserve that woman. She's a good one. And you're a good man. Don't let her out of your grasp."

CHAPTER 31

No matter how insightful and enthusiastic Phil might have been when Price had visited him days ago, Price knew he couldn't just walk in and scoop Fiona off her feet and carry her away.

But, he'd like to think he could woo her again.

Price had never backed down from a challenge—a fight maybe—but not the challenge of getting something he wanted. He'd taken three other skinny, drunk, college kids and made a quartet out of them. Then, somewhere, they added some rock to it. It was unique. It was fun. It became a success.

Shady Joe took off one night and never returned—Phil took his place.

Phil had a decade of experience behind him, and Price sucked in everything the man taught him.

Then he'd met Fiona, and at twenty-three, he knew more than anyone.

Love did that to a man, he thought. It made him soft and dumb—but for all the right reasons.

Now, a man in his fifties, he still loved the same woman. He always had. Oh, others had come and gone in the decade since he'd walked out the door and chosen music over his muse. But no one held a candle to Fiona Gable.

Price opened the door to the coffee shop as they cleaned up for the night. Both Charlie and his fiancée Sadie looked up at him.

"Hello, Mr. Richter," Charlie greeted him. "We're closing up. I can make you a regular coffee, but the rest of the machines are clean for tomorrow."

"Is it brewed already?"

Charlie nodded. "Yes, sir. We brewed off the last bit."

"I'll take a cup."

Charlie went about pouring Price the coffee as Sadie wiped the counter. "How is your friend who was hurt?" she asked.

"He's doing great. They'll let him out in a few days."

She smiled up at him. "That's great news. Will you be leaving then, too?"

Price looked at his arm in the sling. "I have some time still to heal. And, I like it here."

Charlie handed him the cup. "It's on the house," he said.

"Thank you."

"We grew up here," Charlie offered. "It's a nice place to land. It's where my grandparents landed too."

Price nodded. "I met your grandfather once," he said, and Charlie's eyes went wide. "He was a wonderful man."

"Yeah. Wow. You met him?"

Price nodded. "I'd love to tell you about it, if you have time."

Charlie and Sadie exchanged glances and then both nodded. "Let us finish up. We could sit in here, as long as we turn off most of the lights."

Price smiled. "That'll work."

. . .

PULLING OUT A CHAIR, PRICE SAT DOWN AT ONE OF THE TABLES closest to the back of the store. Charlie and Sadie finished cleaning up before turning off the lights over the counter.

Price sipped his strong coffee, wincing at the taste. Well, he hadn't come for coffee. He'd come for a conversation.

Charlie pulled a chair from the table for Sadie, and as she sat, she looked up at him with love in her eyes. Price noticed that Charlie's eyes reciprocated that same love.

Lacing his fingers together, and resting them on the table, Charlie looked up at Price. "When did you meet my grandfather?"

Out of habit, Price picked up the coffee and took a sip. The coffee had grown cold and bitter. He swallowed hard, hoping his face hadn't reacted.

"I met him when I was in my early twenties. I was on a train headed for the coast to audition for a scholarship. To tell you the truth, I can't remember how we even got talking. But we sat together in the observation car for hours. During that time, he told me about his wife and how they'd met and ran off to get married, taking the train until the end of the line."

Charlie smiled. "That's the story my grandmother always told me." He reached for Sadie's hand and interlocked their fingers. "We got engaged after having known one another for two days."

Price couldn't help but laugh out loud. "That's priceless. After meeting your grandfather, his story stayed with me. When I met Fiona, I proposed to her two days later."

Charlie and Sadie exchanged glances. "Really?"

Price nodded. "When I'd met your grandfather, he'd been married to your grandmother for forty years. He was as smitten as you are. I wanted that too. When I met Fi—Fiona," he corrected, "I knew she was it. She said yes, but it took us three years to get married."

"It appears that my grandparents have touched a lot of lives with their story."

"I'd have to agree," Price said, lifting the cup to his lips, then remembering how it tasted, he set it back down. "That's why I'm here. Fiona is embarrassed, and worried, about the book she wrote about your grandparents."

Sadie bit down on her bottom lip. "Ms. Gable said she'd never met Charlie's grandparents."

"She didn't. I gave her the story, just as your grandfather told it to me. I insisted she use the names and descriptions I gave her. At the time, I didn't tell her where I'd gotten the story. Sure, she embellished and wrote the other parts, but the story of their short love affair and elopement, that came from Charlie himself."

"So the story is their story?" Charlie asked.

"It is."

"Wow," Charlie let out a breath. "We thought it was coincidence."

"That's why I wanted to talk to you about it. That book gave Fiona her start. It got her agent, her first book deal, and was a bestseller when it came out. Admittedly, I was just trying to give the woman I loved a muse to follow."

"So why are you sharing this with us?"

Price crossed his legs and sat back in his chair. "She's afraid that your family might sue her, or me."

Charlie's brows drew together. "Why would we do that?"

"Like you said, it's your grandparents' story, and Fiona wrote it."

Charlie nodded slowly. "I don't think my family ever thought much of it."

"I wanted to be honest about it. Fiona doesn't deserve to carry guilt around with her. I'm afraid that if I didn't tell you where the story had come from, well, she'd carry it."

"I can talk to her," Sadie offered. "She comes into the store every day."

"I'll let you two decide what you want to tell her. I just wanted to be clear that I'd met your grandfather and then shared the story with Fiona. His insightfulness changed my life." Price picked up the cup of coffee. "I could use his wisdom now, that's for sure."

"Why?" Charlie ran his fingers through his blond curls.

"I want to get Fi back. I once won her over in two days of meeting her. But it's been ten years since I walked out of her life and eight since we'd spoken. I'd love to have that blind faith again."

Sadie leaned in on her elbows and looked Price right in the eye. "I'm in. How can I help?"

CHAPTER 32

THERE WAS A VASE OF DAISIES ON THE SMALL TABLE SITUATED AT the back of the bookstore where Leona had set Fiona up a place to work each day.

At first, Fiona had fretted that she was in the way and taking up space in Leona's store without paying rent. Leona let her know that she was more than welcome to sit and write her books during business hours for as long as she'd like. Not only did it seem to help Fiona write, being surrounded by books and people, but Leona said she enjoyed Fiona's company. Admittedly, Leona added that sales had gone up since book readers could watch an author hard at work.

Fiona found that refreshingly odd, but her book was coming along—without a happily ever after.

"The daisies spruce up your little corner, I think," Leona complimented as Fiona unpacked her laptop from her backpack.

"It was very thoughtful of you. Thank you."

Leona laughed. "Oh, I didn't put those there. Price did."

Fiona lifted her gaze from the flowers to Leona. "He did?"

"He did."

"Why?"

Leona shrugged. "He came in after you'd left last night and left them for you. He did leave a message for you," she said as she turned to the counter and picked up a folded piece of paper and handed it to Fiona.

Fiona took the note and opened it.

They're dull in comparison to your beauty. Have dinner with me. I'll come by the store at six. Love, Price

"Is this a joke?" she looked up from the note as Sadie walked out of the back room with a cup of tea in her hands.

"Oh, you got Price's note?" Sadie asked.

"I don't understand. Our dinner the other night wasn't successful," Fiona admitted.

"I don't think he feels that way," Sadie sipped her tea.

"Why do you say that?"

"I talked to him. Well, Charlie and I did, last night at the coffee shop."

"He stopped in for coffee?"

"He came in to talk to us as we were closing. He wanted to make it very clear that he was the one that told you the story of Charlie and Ellen, down to the names. I think he was worried that you thought Charlie's family would accuse you of stealing the story."

Fiona's mouth went dry. "He told you that?"

Sadie nodded. "It seemed to be very important to him."

"I had no idea it was a real story when he told me," Fiona's voice shook.

"We know. He met Charlie's grandfather on a train, and they talked. Price said what Charlie's grandfather told him changed his life."

Fiona nodded. "That's what he said to me, too." She rubbed her temples. "I just don't understand why he'd go to you and Charlie. I mean, Phil is better, our dinner was horrible, and it should be time for him to leave. We've been divorced for years now. None of this should matter to him."

Sadie shook her head and rested her hand on Fiona's arm. "Go to dinner with him. I think he'd really like to spend time with you."

Fiona narrowed her eyes on her. "Did he say that?"

Sadie sipped her tea, again. "He's a sweet guy, and I think he misses you."

Biting down on her bottom lip to keep it from quivering, Fiona looked down at the note. Could he possibly miss her—really? They'd gone their separate ways years ago. The dreams they once had, together, never materialized, and they chose their careers over a lifetime together.

She supposed she could give him an hour, or two. Though she wasn't sure what good it would do.

FIONA FOUND IT INTERESTING THAT BOTH LEONA AND SADIE WERE busy working at six o'clock, when they'd usually be locked up and finalizing the paperwork for the day. In fact, Sadie would typically be working at the coffee shop in the evenings with her fiancé.

No doubt both women were looking to see how Fiona was going to react to Price showing up.

And why shouldn't they be a little curious? Fiona had disappeared at four o'clock to run an errand, and had come back to the store with her hair and makeup done, as well as having changed her clothes.

Sure, they hadn't said anything, but she knew they'd noticed.

Promptly, at six o'clock, Price walked through the door, and immediately, Fiona noticed that both of his arms were though the sleeves of his coat.

"You're out of your arm brace," Sadie said as he walked toward the counter. "I'll bet that's a relief."

Price smiled and nodded. "It is. It's sore and my mobility

sucks. I have to be mindful of it, and the sling goes back on at night. But for now, I'm free."

His gaze shifted from Sadie to Fiona. She swallowed hard as his smile resurfaced, and this time he aimed it at her.

Price closed the space between them. "You look beautiful," he said, his gaze never leaving her eyes.

"Thank you. Are you ready?" she asked, pulling her coat from the back of the chair and hoping to make a quick exit. The hopefulness in the eyes of Sadie and Leona was starting to make Fiona's head spin.

Price helped her with her coat, and then, with his hand pressed to the small of her back, he escorted her to the door.

"I'll have her back before curfew," he teased, calling back to the women who had giddy smiles on their faces.

When the door closed behind them, Fiona took a deliberate step to distance herself from him. "They didn't need the whole show."

"Sure they did. Didn't you see their faces?" He mused, tucking his hands into his pockets.

"Don't make this awkward."

Now his eyes had narrowed on her. "There's nothing awkward about this, Fi. It's us. We were never awkward."

Her skin heated under her coat. What exactly was that supposed to mean, and why had she reacted?

Blowing out a warm breath into the frigid air, Fiona willed herself to calm. There was no reason to be nervous, scared, or irritated. He was right. They'd never been awkward around each other. They'd split and distanced themselves before it could become awkward.

She and Price had a history. Now that he was healing, he could go on his way. For the rest of the night, she'd just consider this his farewell party.

CHAPTER 33

WALKING SIDE BY SIDE, KEEPING HIS HANDS IN HIS POCKETS, PRICE walked Fiona to the parking lot where his rental car had been parked.

Pushing the button on the fob in his pocket, the lights of the Buick flashed, and he reached to open her door.

"You have a car here?" she asked.

"I rented one. I didn't realize I'd be here this long," he said as she slid into the seat, and he closed the door.

Price rounded the car, pulled open the door, and climbed in behind the steering wheel. He started the car, and quickly adjusted the volume of the radio before the heat.

"I was getting inspired," he chuckled at the thought that the volume on the radio had been blasting before he'd driven to the bookstore. "Are you warm enough?"

"I'll be fine," Fiona said curtly.

He wasn't going to take it personally. He figured by the end of the night he'd have made her mad a handful of times, but if everything went according to plan, maybe she'd be mad wrapped in his arms.

Price backed out of the parking space and Fiona looked around. "Where are we going?"

Price smiled. "I thought we'd check in on an old friend."

He could see her push back into the seat, her hands clasped together in her lap. Surely she'd figured out where he was taking her, and he assumed she was okay with going, as she hadn't argued. But, the thought made her nervous. That was obvious.

Biting down on the inside of his cheek to keep the smile from surfacing, Price was humored by her. There was an argument brewing in her head, he knew. She wanted to be mad that he was even considering taking her to see Phil. On the other hand, Phil had been her friend too, and he knew she was worried about him —and worried about seeing him.

She'd be mad after, but for now, she'd fume in the seat next to him.

What did it matter, he considered, as long as she was right there with him.

"How's the new book coming along?" he asked and noticed Fiona's grip ease as she brushed her hands over her lap, then adjusted her scarf.

"Fine. Good."

For a woman who used words to make a living, he found it humorous when they failed her.

"It's nice that they set you up a little workspace. I think Leona enjoys having you there."

Fiona turned her head toward him. "I didn't thank you for the flowers."

"I thought you needed a little sunshine."

"Well, thank you. It was quite a surprise." She gripped her hands together again. "You also spoke to Charlie and Sadie?"

Price gripped the steering wheel tighter. "I did. You were worried about me telling you Charlie McGowan's story, and I didn't want that to be an issue for you."

"For me?"

"Yes."

"You didn't do that for your own reasons? You're the one that told me the story. You're the one that suggested the names. You're the one..."

"Who loved you so much, I wanted to see you succeed with the story you built around it." He shifted a glance in her direction, and she shifted hers out the window. "They were very cordial about it. Charlie McGowan was a fine man who loved his wife and had an amazing romance. You shared that romance with the entire world, and we shared a lot of great years because of his encouragement to me."

She didn't seem to have anything else to say, and he let her have her silence as he drove toward the hospital.

Price pulled into the parking lot of the hospital and parked the car. They sat in awkward silence for a moment, before Price cleared his throat.

"Ready to go in?" he asked, and Fiona turned toward him, her eyes damp.

"I'm sorry," she said faintly.

He hadn't expected that. "Do you have something to be sorry for?"

"You're trying to be kind and I keep snapping out the same arguments at you."

Okay, so she'd had some kind of come-to-God moment. He'd take it.

"I'm not offended by you being angry at me. You've had a lot of years to store that up."

"I did a good job of it."

He couldn't help but chuckle at that. "Let's go see Phil. He'll get a kick out of seeing you."

Fiona rested her hand on his, and he drew in the warmth from it. "Is he bad? What am I walking into?"

Price, needing to feel her touch, placed his hand over hers, so she wouldn't pull away. "Considering what he's been through, he looks good. They had to shave his head and do surgery to relieve the pressure of blood on his brain," he said and watched as she flinched. "He's got a long recovery ahead of him, but he remembers things and can talk. That's a big deal."

She blew out a breath. "Do you think he'll know who I am?"

"He'll know you."

"I'm nervous."

Price patted her hand. "I'll be right there with you."

With her free hand, she wiped away the tears that had escaped and rolled down her cheeks.

THEY STEPPED OUT OF THE CAR, AND FIONA NOTICED HOW gingerly Price moved.

"Are you sure you shouldn't be wearing that brace still?"

The corner of his mouth curled up. "They said I'm fine, and to just take it easy."

"Like when you sprained your ankle?" she scolded. "Six weeks on crutches and you refused."

"I'm older now. I heed warnings better," he teased.

Fiona let out a grunt. "Why don't I believe you?"

He moved toward her, his uninjured arm moving behind her, and his hand pressing on the small of her back as they walked toward the hospital.

"Because you know me better than anyone in the world."

She bit down on her lip. "I did know you…"

"You do," he said definitely.

CHAPTER 34

Sickness swept through Fiona as they stopped in front of Phil's door. She pressed her hands to her stomach and closed her eyes, willing herself to breathe.

"Are you okay?" Price's voice was soft as he touched her hands.

Fiona opened her eyes. "I hate hospitals."

"I know you do," he said, and she realized that he knew her—or had known her—better than anyone in the world. "Just take a few breaths before we go in. Phil knows you hate them too, and he'll see that by the pasty color of your skin."

"Maybe I shouldn't go in," she said just as the door opened and Rosalyn let out a little squeak.

"I didn't know there was anyone out here," she said, pressing her hand to her chest. "Hey, Price." She leaned into him and kissed him right on the lips. "He has a lot of fire and piss in him tonight."

"Almost his old self, huh?"

They shared a laugh. "He'll be happy you're here. I think he's tired of me fussing over him."

"Are you headed out?"

Rosalyn shook her head. "I'm going to go get some dinner and shut my eyes in the waiting room for a bit with my headphones on."

"He's glad you're here," Price assured her.

"Yeah. He's awfully forgiving," she sighed on a breath and then lifted her head to look at Fiona as if she hadn't noticed her standing there before. "I'm being rude. I'm sorry. I'm Rosalyn, Phil's—" she paused. "Oh, my goodness. Fiona?"

Fiona nodded hesitantly, still not sure she had enough air in her lungs to speak.

But there was no time for words. Rosalyn moved to her and enveloped her in a hug.

"What are you doing here? What are you doing here with him?" she teased as she pulled back at arm's length and studied Fiona. "You look amazing. God, I'm jealous. How did you age so beautifully? And by age, I just mean, well, we're women of a certain age, you know what I mean. You look fantastic. Oh, and your newest book. Ah-mazing," she emphasized the word.

Fiona battled the sickness swirling in her belly and the tears that threatened, along with the laughter bubbling in her chest.

The laughter escaped first, thankfully. "Thank you. You're very sweet."

"What are you doing here?" she asked again.

"I live here now. It's all coincidence," Fiona said, and Rosalyn nodded slowly with a hum.

"Is it now?" She shifted a look in Price's direction. "You didn't tell me she was here?" Before he could answer, Rosalyn turned back to Fiona. "These boys don't say enough of the right things, but the wrong things are abundant."

She took Fiona's arm and started back into the room.

"C'mon. He'll flip to see you."

Fiona shot Price a worried glance, only to see him smile wide. Jerk! she thought.

"Look who I found in the hallway," Rosalyn announced as she walked into the room.

That sickness swirled harder in Fiona's stomach and threatened to take her to her knees.

From what she knew of the accident, it had been weeks ago, but she didn't think Phil looked good. So how bad had he been if this was looking great.

"He dragged you here? Isn't it my lucky day?" Phil smiled up at her and reached his hand out for her to take it.

"I'm going to go eat," Rosalyn said as she moved in and kissed Phil on the lips, as she had to Price, then made her exit.

Fiona took Phil's offered hand and stepped closer to the bed. "How are you?" her voice cracked.

"I'm dancing a jig, can't you tell?"

She wasn't sure if that was humor or anger, but when Price laughed behind her, and then Phil did the same, she assumed it was his humor.

"You look great. Price said you did."

Fiona swallowed hard. "He did?"

"Of course. His eyes still twinkle when he talks about you," Phil admitted, and Price moved from behind her and walked toward the chair on the other side of the room.

"I'm standing right here. No need to tell her all my secrets," Price teased as he pulled off his coat and draped it over the chair.

He walked back to her and urged her out of her coat before he pulled up the other chair and placed it next to the bed.

"Sit down before your knees lock," he said softly.

Fiona did as instructed.

"You still hate these places, huh?" Phil chuckled.

"Yes."

"Me too. It won't be long, and I'll be out of here. Then off to a rehab center to work on walking and all that stuff."

"You have to do that?"

"I lost some motor skills. My mouth still runs and my

memory works, so I'm counting that as a win," he boasted. "And you saw Ros. She came back to me, and she don't look like she's going anywhere else." Phil sighed and smiled. "This might have been the best thing that ever happened to all of us."

Fiona looked over at Price, who rubbed an ache from his shoulder, and smiled at her.

What a horrible thought, Fiona considered. When was a tragedy something to welcome?

Then again, she supposed it wasn't so tragic. The band was beaten and bruised. Perhaps now the band was done, as Price had hinted at. Their perspectives had changed.

Forgiveness had been found, she realized too.

If Phil could forgive Rosalyn, perhaps she could give Price the few moments he'd been seeking to become friends again.

"When are you going to get to go home? I mean back to your home?" Fiona asked, knowing that Price wouldn't go anywhere until Phil did.

"Wherever Ros is, that's home. Right now, that's here. Maybe I can convince her to stick around, and we can start over. Just like I hear you're doing."

Fiona nodded. "You'd start over here?"

"Seems like a nice place. Quiet. Coffee shop is cute," he laughed. "It's time to embrace the life I got a second chance at with the woman I never stopped loving."

Now Fiona's lip quivered as she shifted a quick glance toward Price, who smiled at her.

Well, this wasn't how she thought her new start at life was going to go. Whatever she'd thought she'd been escaping by moving, had followed her.

Fiona drew in a breath. Would that new story she was working on actually have a happily ever after?

CHAPTER 35

FIONA AND PRICE WALKED BACK TO HIS CAR. FIONA WRAPPED HER arms around herself to fight off the cold and to steady herself.

Price unlocked the car and opened her door for her.

Just as she moved to slide in, he pulled her to him, their noses nearly touching.

"You're awfully quiet," he said, the scent of his cologne intoxicating her.

"I guess I have a lot on my mind," Fiona admitted.

Price lifted his hand to her cheek, brushing his calloused fingertips over her skin.

"There's a lot happening right now, and I assume you moved here for some peace and quiet."

"I did."

"That doesn't seem to be happening."

As if it were possible, Price stepped even closer to her.

"Fi, I believe in fate," he said softly, his breath hanging in the cold air.

"Price..."

His thumb brushed her quivering lips. "Don't tell me you've lost that part of you. The part that throws caution to the wind.

The part that believes that it's okay to jump into something feet first. The part that always believed in second chances."

"I don't know what I believe," she admitted.

In the past ten years, Fiona had indeed lost those parts of her. When they'd chosen their careers over their marriage, she'd let her life become one sorrowful moment after another—hence the move to start over.

What would her twenty-year-old self say to Price now?

Price gingerly rested his hand on her hip, wincing at the pain that must have caused his shoulder to move in that direction.

"I think you believe in fate too," he said, brushing the tips of their noses together. "I think that Phil made you reconsider hating me."

"I don't hate you."

His cheeks rose as he smiled. "I didn't think so."

Price's lips came to hers and pressed against them. Fiona couldn't help but to lean into him and part her lips to absorb his kiss.

The familiarity of it rushed back at her, causing a surge of heat to rise from her toes to the top of her head. The same rush came to her as it had that first time he'd kissed her when she was still in college.

Every moment they'd shared together flashed behind her closed eyelids. This man—oh this man, she thought.

Instinct took over as much as need, and Fiona gripped the front of Price's coat, urging him even closer.

The kiss deepened and the swirl of heat being created hung in the air.

Fiona lifted her arms around Price's neck, and he quickly pulled back and winced.

Fiona broke from him, covering her mouth with her hands.

"I'm sorry. I'm so sorry," she stammered.

"It's nothing. It's okay," he assured her. "Seriously, it's okay."

"I didn't mean to hurt you."

He chuckled and readjusted. "You could never hurt me, Fi."

She wasn't so sure of that.

"C'mon," he said. "Let's get out of the cold and go have dinner."

Fiona nodded and slid into the car.

"But, Fi," Price began and Fiona looked up at him. "I'm not done here. Start thinking about after dinner. I'm not asking for all night. But I'd like to explore that just a little more."

Price shut the door and Fiona rested her head back.

What was she doing?

Oh, she knew what she was doing. She was falling in love all over again—only this time she wasn't twenty. This time they wouldn't be heartbroken when kids didn't come their way. This time he wouldn't leave her to travel for weeks.

Her stomach knotted.

This wasn't what she'd been looking for when she moved.

Then again, what had she been looking for?

CHAPTER 36

THEY'D DRIVEN TO THREE RESTAURANTS THAT HAD HOUR-LONG wait times. Even the local drive-in burger place had cars waiting.

Price scanned each side of the street as he drove. For a cold Friday in February, everyone seemed to have left home in search of warmth and other people.

"Maybe dinner is out of the question," Fiona said as she too turned her head to look out the window at the lines at the doors of each restaurant.

Price nodded and then laughed. "I have an idea."

She turned to him. "What?"

"Do you trust me?"

He saw her bite down on her lip. "I always have."

"It won't be good, but it'll be memorable."

Price turned at the next corner and then pulled into the 7-11 parking lot. "Give me five minutes."

Fiona laughed, and her eyes lit in the darkness of the car. "I should come in and help you."

Price shook his head. "I'll manage."

He climbed out of the car, leaving it running, and shut the

door behind him. Because he knew her well enough, he listened, and heard the lock on the door engage.

Price walked into the crowded convenience store and began to gather items.

He knew the smile on his face was wide. He couldn't help it.

Their first date had gone much the same way, thirty-some years ago. They couldn't get into a restaurant they could afford, and they'd ended up with chips, cooked items from the roller display, and Slurpees.

The options on the roller display had gotten only slightly better in thirty years.

Price laid his items on the counter and picked up a two pack of cupcakes for dessert. As the woman behind the counter, whose name was Marian according to her name tag, rang him up, Price chuckled to himself. If this didn't win her back, he wasn't sure what would.

Marian put the items in a bag, and skillfully, Price looped the bag over his tender wrist, and balanced the Slurpee tray in the other hand.

Knowing he couldn't balance everything to open his car door, he walked to the passenger side of the car. Fiona rolled down the window, and he was sure the smile on her face matched his.

"Oh, this is old school, huh?" she laughed as she took the bag from him and set it at her feet before she took the tray of drinks from him.

"Back to basics," Price said with a wink as he skirted the front of the car and climbed back inside. "Now, where do we take our elegant dining experience? Your place or mine?"

The smile had faded from Fiona's lips.

Price didn't much like the fact that she seemed to go sad and quiet.

"Or, we can eat it right here in the car," he offered.

Fiona lifted her eyes to meet his. "You have a place here?"

"I knew Phil's recovery was going to take a long time. I got a short-term rental for a few months. So, yes, I have a place."

She chewed her lip. "And when you don't live here, where do you live?"

"San Francisco," he said softly, knowing how much she loved it there.

"I'll bet that's nice."

"It was. I'm growing rather fond of it here though."

She looked down at the tray she held on her lap. "It's a nice place, but not near a metropolis or big music venues. There's not a recording studio here that I know of. There is only one coffee shop and one bookstore."

"And it's the most charming city I've ever been to," he said before she could say anything more. "Let's circle back to, yes, I have a place."

"Let's go to my place," she offered.

"I would like that," Price backed out of the lot and pulled to the stop sign. "Which way do I go?"

As he waited, Fiona took a deep breath, and he knew she was trying to convince herself that it was okay—of course, Price was all in. He had a mission now, and that bag of crap from 7-11 was only his ticket in the door. He had to make her swoon.

"Go right. We're not too far."

FIONA HELD TIGHTLY TO THE DRINKS IN HER LAP. SHE WAS INVITING Price into her home—her private sanctuary. He was about to see her home—sans anything Price Richter.

It had taken eight years and a few moves to erase twenty plus years of marriage, but she'd done it when she'd come here.

Maybe it was all a big mistake to take Price home—as much of a mistake as kissing him at the hospital. No, that was no mistake. That had been chemistry, and they'd never had a problem fueling that.

Fiona had eighteen blocks to decide what she wanted from the night, because once she let him into her home, she knew she had to be sure of what she wanted. If she was ready to reconcile, then her new move to a new town included Price. He'd be part of her life for the rest of her life.

But if it wasn't what she wanted, then she needed to make that decision before they ever got out of the car.

He'd chosen his career—and she'd made it so easy for him to walk away.

No matter how hard she'd tried over the years to replace him, it hadn't worked. The romance author didn't understand romance and love—well, not anymore, that was.

No man held a candle to Price Richter, so she doubted beyond tonight anyone ever would.

"I'm just driving here," his voice broke her thoughts. "You have to tell me where to go."

"Right. Sorry." She looked up. "Turn here," she said quickly, pointing to the corner only a few feet from them.

Price slowed quickly and made the turn. Fiona held tightly to the drinks in her lap, and kept the bag at her feet steady.

"Take the next right, and I'm the house at the end of the cul-de-sac."

Price nodded and drove in the direction Fiona had led him.

"This is cute," he said as he pulled up to the house and parked the car in the driveway. "Nice little bungalow, huh?"

"It was the right price at the right time."

"More fate, I think. I haven't even been inside, and I can tell that it's just your style."

Fiona forced a strained smile to her lips. It was just her style. All her style and no one else's. Would he notice, she wondered?

Well, perhaps she'd wait to make her decision on what she wanted from Price until he'd been into her little sanctuary. Maybe he wouldn't want to stay at all.

CHAPTER 37

FIONA UNLOCKED THE DOOR AND CARRIED THE TRAY WITH THE Slurpees into the house. She flipped on the light switch, illuminating the entrance as they walked in.

She heard Price chuckle behind her, and she turned to watch him cross the threshold.

"I hate to say it," he drew in a deep breath. "I've missed all of those scented things you used to have around the house."

Fiona drew in a breath as well. She'd become so used to her scents that she found comfort in them, but they no longer stood out to her. It had however, been a point of many of their arguments. Fiona loved scented candles, oils, lotions, and laundry soaps. Price had never been a fan of her obsession. When he'd traveled, she'd light candles from the moment he left until two days before he came back. That way, the scents dissipated before he returned.

"Will it bother you?"

Price shook his head. "No. This is your home, and it smells like you."

She wasn't sure how to take that, but she assumed it was a compliment, of sorts.

Fiona led him through the living and dining area toward the kitchen, which was situated at the back of the house. She could feel him looking around as they walked through the house.

"This is a nice place, Fi."

She turned on the kitchen light and set the drinks on the table. Turning to reach for the bag Price carried, she noticed his smile.

"You still have my grandmother's kitchen table?" he asked.

Fiona looked at the table, and then back up at him. "Yes," she said flatly. "You're always welcome to it. It's yours after all."

His smile widened. "It means a lot that you kept it."

"It's a nice table," she said, knowing it was the only thing in the house that they'd once shared.

Fiona shrugged off her coat and scarf, hanging it on the back of one of the chairs. Price followed and did the same.

She turned to take the paper towel roll from the holder, and before she could turn back around, she felt Price's hands come to her hips. His body pressed to hers, and his lips skimmed the sensitive skin on her neck.

Her knees went weak, and she set down the paper towels, and held on to the counter for support.

"Price…"

"I said I wasn't done," he whispered into her neck.

Fiona turned into his embrace, her back pressed to the counter. She was careful not to touch his shoulder. Instead, she wrapped her arms around him as he lifted his hand into her hair.

"You're so beautiful," Price said.

"Price…"

"I mean it," he said, pressing his lips to her neck and she let her head roll back. "I've never known a woman more beautiful."

"I'm not who I was a decade ago," she said breathlessly.

"Neither am I," Price admitted as he skimmed his lips over her collarbone. "And that's a good thing. Obviously, who we were a decade ago, well…"

He hadn't finished what he was saying. Instead, he lifted his lips to Fiona's and took her under with a kiss that scrambled her thoughts.

FIONA'S MOUTH WAS SOFT AND WARM. JUST THE MEMORY OF HER kisses had pulled him through some dark nights. And now, here he was, in her home with her in his arms. It was surreal. He'd always believed in fate, and he was sure that was what had happened between them to bring them to this moment. Perhaps it was fate that they'd been divorced as long as they had, and somehow, he had her in his arms now.

Fiona eased back. "We'd better eat this fancy dinner," she said breathlessly.

Price kept his eyes closed for another moment and held her near. "I'm so glad you're here," he said.

"You don't think this is a little crazy?"

He opened his eyes and shook his head. "Everything has a reason, Fi. Everything."

"Even car accidents?"

"Everything," he repeated softly before kissing her once more.

Fiona moved from him, picking up the paper towel roll. He watched her as she walked to the table and sat down. Phil was right, Price thought Fiona at this age, was still the most beautiful woman he'd ever seen in his entire life.

He desperately wanted to tell her what was stirring in him— the need to keep her near, and to tell her he still loved her.

He watched as she pulled the items from the bag and laughed. "We're going to end up with Type II Diabetes."

"Not from one meal, Fi," he said, moving to the table and placing his hands on the back of a chair.

"You got cupcakes?"

"Do you still like them?"

Her lips curled up in a knowing grin, and she didn't give him a verbal answer. He didn't need one.

"Do you want the Doritos or the regular chips?" she held up the two bags.

"Why don't we pour them both out and share?"

She nodded. "And what came off the roller?"

Price laughed now too. "I have no idea. Maybe an egg roll, some pizza thing. I think there is a hot dog."

Her nose wrinkled up. "I can't believe we used to eat this stuff all the time."

"It was all we could afford."

She lifted her eyes to meet his. "I guess we have come a long way, haven't we?"

"My retirement fund is well padded," he admitted, in case it made a difference.

"So is mine," she admitted. "*A Winter in Connecticut* has a producer looking into movie rights."

Price moved toward her and touched her arm. "Fi, that's amazing."

"It's not a done deal."

"It's still amazing. You've always wanted that."

Fiona leveled her eyes with his. "They also want Ellen and Charlie's story. It wasn't a big deal until I met Sadie and Charlie. Now I don't know if I want something that big to happen to that book."

Price felt a twisting in his gut. He understood that.

"They wanted Fiona's Wedding Song for a movie once," he said, picking up a straw and tearing off the paper. "I wouldn't let it go. No one plays or sings that song but me."

"And all of your fans on YouTube and TikTok?"

Price grinned. "Impersonation is the best form of flattery?"

"So they say."

Price pulled out a chair and sat down.

"I'm happy for you, Fi. I'm really happy for you."

"Thank you."

He put the straw he'd opened into her Slurpee and then repeated the process with his own. He lifted his up and held it out toward her.

"To big dreams that are becoming reality. To the health, recovery and well-being of our friends. To towns with crazy stories. And for us, Fi. May we never know another day apart."

CHAPTER 38

FIONA SET DOWN HER DRINK BECAUSE HER HAND SHOOK, AND SHE knew it wasn't from the cold drink.

May we never know another day apart, his words rang in her ears.

Price must have noticed that what he said had stirred her up because he reached for her hand and covered it with his own.

"Fi?"

"This is—I don't know what all of this is."

"Fate."

She stood, paced, and raked her fingers through her hair. "You have to stop saying that. I haven't talked to you in eight years. You can't tell me that for eight years you simply pined for me again. I never spoke to you," she said again.

Price lowered his head. "You're right. I chose my career and touring. I picked the opportunities that came my way over my marriage. I was selfish."

It surprised her, and she lifted her head to look at him.

He stood and moved toward her. "I tried to move on from you. I tried to forget what we had. I might have even been good at it for a while. And then I'd walk by some bookstore or turn on

167

the TV to some talk show, and there was your face, your books, your words."

Price reached a hand to her arm. "Let me guess, you turned off more music than you cared to. You walked out of stores that had music in the background. You'd hum your wedding song and then hate yourself for it."

Fiona knew her eyes went wide.

A smile formed on his lips and he looked resigned.

"I don't want to be done being with you—in general. I'm not leaving until Phil leaves. He's a priority for me. So I'll be around, Fi. I sure would like to be here with you. But, I understand that we have hurt each other enough that there are hang-ups." He looked back at the table of melting drinks and cold food. "I'll see myself out."

He reached for his coat and she stopped him. What was she doing?

"No," she heard her voice tremble. "Don't go. Don't let me push you away—again."

Price studied her for a moment, scanning a look over her. "Don't go?"

"I love you," her voice hiccupped. "I have always loved you, and I've missed you every minute of every day that I haven't been with you." Fiona sucked in a breath, and touched a trembling hand to her lips. "We were a family, even if it was just you and me. We suffered together. We won together. We celebrated, together." Tears rolled down her cheeks.

His eyes lightened as he moved to her and rested his hands on her hips. "You love me?"

She nodded and sniffed. "Price, it all hurts having you here because I've always loved you and waited to have those feelings again—for you—for someone."

He lifted his good arm and brushed away tears from her cheek with his thumb. "I've always loved you too, Fi. It hurt sometimes something awful. I read your books, and I knew you were hurting. But I knew you believed in happily ever after. You wrote about it, and you never wrote a thing you didn't believe in."

Her breath shuttered. "What do we do? How do we go forward? How do we forgive and forget?"

"We don't forget."

"We forgive?"

He nodded and pressed his forehead to hers. "Forgive me, Fi. Forgive me for choosing myself over us."

She nodded, her forehead rubbing against his. "I forgive you. Forgive me?"

He let out a breath. "I forgive you. I love you, Fi."

"I love you too."

Price eased back and looked down at her. "Okay, we're here now. Right where we were over thirty years ago when I saw you standing at the side of the stage, a clipboard in your hand, and a stage pass around your neck."

She laughed. "God, I volunteered for everything back then."

"Because you cared and wanted to be involved." He reminded her, brushing a strand of hair from her forehead. "I just remember singing every song to you, because I couldn't take my eyes off of you. I knew, Fi. I knew at that moment you were my forever."

"You proposed two days later."

"And you said yes. You knew we belonged together. You knew it was fate to take that volunteer job, Fi. Tell me you still believe in fate. Just like Charlie and Ellen believed in it, and I'd followed suit."

Her lip quivered, and she bit down on it to stop it.

Price stepped back, and with a hand on the back of one of the chairs, he lowered himself down on one knee.

Another flood of tears broke through, and Fiona covered her mouth with both hands.

"I love you, Fi. I've never stopped. I've lived with regret for years." He reached for her hand and then pressed a kiss to the back of it. "We knew then. We knew so fast that we were meant to be together. We're there again. Forever is within our grasp. Understanding commitment and give and takes comes with age. Forgiveness is easier too."

She wiped her cheeks with her free hand. Her heart hammered in her chest and she could hardly breathe.

"Fi," Price said softly. "Marry me, Fi. Marry me again and let's start all over. Marry me and love me forever."

Words wouldn't surface. She knew her answer, but it wouldn't come out.

Pulling her hand from Price, she walked away and down the hallway.

"Fi," he called after her.

She hurried to her bedroom, turned on the lights, and pulled open her closet door. She stepped inside and began to pull boxes from the shelf.

"Fiona," his voice was at the door to her room. "I'll go. I'll go now. I'm sorry," he began and stopped as she turned with the box in her hands that she'd been looking for.

Tears still streamed down her cheeks as she set the box on the bed.

"Fi?"

She shook her head and sniffed back tears as she opened the box full of twenty plus years of memories of their life together. Ultrasound photos, flowers, concert tickets, love notes, they all spilled out onto the bed as she dumped the box and sorted through it until she found the small box she'd been looking for.

Price picked up one of the ultrasound photos, and she heard him sniff back tears too.

Then she turned to him, the small box in her hand.

Words still wouldn't come. Breath would hardly surface, and her head was spinning.

Price put the ultrasound photo down and looked at Fiona's shaking hands.

She opened the box and took out the two familiar rings inside.

"Oh, Fi."

She dropped the box on the bed, but held the rings in her hand. Handing Price the ring he'd once put on her finger, she held out the gold band she'd put on his finger all those years ago.

She took his hand and pushed the ring on his finger as far as it would go, and then with humor in her heart, she looked up at him.

"I'm a little heavier than I was eight years ago when I took it off," he said as he sniffed back tears.

Fiona laughed and moved the ring to his pinkie.

Price looked down at the ring he held between his fingers. "Does this mean you'll marry me?"

Fiona looked up at him, her vision clouded by the tears that wouldn't go away. "Yes," she whispered. "Yes."

Price took the ring he held in his hand and tried to slide it on her finger too, only to get past the first knuckle.

Laughter erupted between them as he took the ring and slid it onto her pinkie.

"I love you, Fi. It won't be like the last time, I promise. It'll be better. I'm ready to work on it being better."

CHAPTER 39

They'd fallen into a heap on the floor. Arms, legs, and lips tangled together until they'd eventually fallen asleep in one another's arms. With rings on their fingers, they'd promised to start over. They'd promised to continue to love one another forever. They'd promised to choose love over any individual need.

Two heads lifted in unison when Fiona walked into the bookstore on Saturday morning. She didn't assume she'd walked in every other morning brooding, but today, both Leona and Sadie studied her.

"Good morning, Fiona," Leona's voice was nearly sing-song like. "I didn't expect to see you this morning. You don't usually come in on Saturdays."

"I just came to visit."

Leona nodded her head slowly. "There's hot water in the electric pot if you want some tea."

"Thank you." Fiona walked toward the back room, filled a mug, and decided on peppermint tea because it matched her mood.

When she returned to the store, both women were perched on high stools, and had one waiting for Fiona.

She set her mug down on the counter and shrugged out of her coat. Hanging her coat on the rack near the counter, she walked back and sat on the stool. She picked up her mug, and sipped.

"You look like the cat that ate the canary," Leona said, her mug poised at her lips.

"Do I?"

"Your date went well then?"

"Hmmm? Oh, yeah, it was good."

Sadie studied her and then Leona. "Where did you go?"

"7-11."

There was a silence between them all before Leona chuckled and Sadie followed.

"Romantic," Leona said, sipped, and then studied Fiona's hand. "New hardware?"

"What's that?"

Leona set her mug down and reached for Fiona's hand. "Fiona, what is this?"

Fiona tucked her lips between her teeth to steady her smiled. "That would be my wedding ring. Doesn't quite fit right."

"You could have it altered."

"Yes, I think I might."

Sadie shifted looks between the women again. "What does it mean?" she nearly shouted.

Now Fiona smiled wide. "It means in honor of how we first did things, Price and I have decided, rather quickly, to get married and start over."

Anyone nearby would have thought the store was filled with excited teenagers by the sound of squeals and hollering that went on when Sadie and Leona hopped from their stools and pulled Fiona into them.

"I'm so happy for you," Leona said gleefully.

"Thank you."

"Charlie will be so happy," Sadie said as she hugged Fiona and eased back.

"He will?" Fiona laughed.

Sadie nodded. "He knew. He just knew his grandfather's legacy and words were still resonating with Price. He just knew it would happen again."

Well, Fiona thought, how could she argue with the legacy of Charlie McGowan—the older one.

~

ROSALYN LIFTED HER HEAD WHEN PRICE PUSHED OPEN THE DOOR to Phil's room.

"Hey," she said softly.

"Hey," Price returned and looked at the empty room. "They kicked him out but kept you?"

She laughed easily. "PT."

"So he's up and moving?"

She nodded, and her eyes welled with tears. "He's doing great."

Price watched as she batted her eyes and bit down on her lip. Moving to her, he knelt down in front of her. "So why are you crying?"

"How much of all of this was trauma? I mean, I packed a bag and flew out here the second I heard. I left my life frozen back home to come here. Now, he's almost better."

"And that's a good thing. I also think he's doing so well because you're here."

"Yeah, well, this part is almost over, right? Then you'll all start going on the road again, and I'll go back to my life. It's just—well, it's just the next step."

Price gathered Rosalyn's hands in his. "Is that what you want?"

She shook her head. "I want to be with him. I broke up our marriage. I know that. But, I love him."

"He loves you too," Price assured her. "He'll go wherever you are. And for the record, I think we're done touring."

"Does he know that?"

"I know that," Phil's voice came from the door as a nurse wheeled him back into the room.

Rosalyn wiped her cheeks and forced a shaky smile to her lips as Price stood.

"So, you're walking?"

The nurse laughed first, and resigned to it, Phil did as well. "I'm, toddling."

"That's the first move, right?"

The nurse parked the wheelchair next to the bed and helped Phil transfer. She situated him on the bed, entered information on the computer, and then left the room.

"I'll be free in two days, they say," Phil adjusted himself on the bed. "I'm going stir crazy."

"You look good though, pal."

"I feel good," he said, reaching his hand out toward Rosalyn.

She looked up at him, stood, and took his hand.

"I couldn't have done it without this beautiful woman by my side."

Rosalyn shook her head. "Stop."

"Seriously, you've been my rock. I think you should think about sticking it out," Phil said, and she lifted her eyes to him.

"Yeah?"

"Yeah," he said. "Let's lay down some new roots here. Price is doing it."

Rosalyn looked up at Price, and he nodded, holding up his left hand and flashing the gold band on his pinkie. "I got engaged last night," he laughed and even Phil adjusted to look at him better.

"No, kidding?" Phil's voice lifted in tone.

"No kidding. The first time, I proposed in two days. I didn't see any reason to wait to start over. She said yes."

Rosalyn's damp eyes brightened, and she walked around the bed to hug him. "I'm happy for you."

"Thanks."

"Well, now you're just one-upping me," Phil complained. "I don't have rings."

"This is the original. You can see it doesn't fit."

"Hmmm," Phil grunted and contorted his lips into a pucker. "We didn't even have rings."

Rosalyn grinned. "A little too hippy for that."

Phil sat up straighter and reached for Rosalyn. "You're right. We're a little too hippy for that, but I'd buy you the biggest rock or shiniest piece of gold in the world if you wanted it."

"I don't."

"Then you'll take just me and a lame ass proposal?" Her eyes went wide. "Stick around, Ros? Hitch your wagon to mine again? Let's start all over, right here in this place—and we'll know a couple of people."

Her lips trembled. "Really?"

"Yeah."

"You forgive me for everything I've—"

"Ros, I never blamed you. I love you. That's all I have to offer."

"I love you, too," she swallowed a sob and moved in to kiss him.

Price drew in an audible breath. "Well, I came to share my news, and I guess I'll go."

Rosalyn laughed as she pulled back from Phil. "I'm really happy for you and Fiona."

Price nodded. "And I'm happy for the two of you as well. It looks like we'll all get our happily ever after."

CHAPTER 40

FIONA FLITTED AROUND THE KITCHEN THAT A WEEK AGO WAS ALL hers. She'd been happy alone in her new house, starting over, but she was over the moon to have Price there with her.

They'd had their rings sized, and now hers sparkled up at her from the correct finger.

She sensed Price before he moved behind her and wrapped his arms around her waist. "You have everything put together. Stop fussing," he said.

"I haven't had people in my house. Our house," she corrected. "I hadn't realized I'd amassed so many friends," she laughed.

"Five, Fi. We only have five people coming over."

"For dinner and a wedding they don't know about."

He turned her in his arms. "I like it better this way. You, me, a couple of friends, and an official document to sign."

She shook her head and smiled, then rested her head on his shoulder.

"I didn't expect this to happen to me. I might have written it in a book—but not in my life."

"It belongs in your life," he said as the doorbell rang. "I'll get that."

He left her alone in the kitchen. Fiona turned and gripped the counter for support. He was right. It did belong in her life.

She could hear the conversations from the other room. Everyone had arrived at the same time.

There was no better time to get married than surrounded by the friends made, and those they'd had, in the town where they'd both, by chance, landed.

Fiona walked to the living room and Leona moved to her, pulling her in for a hug. "This is the cutest house I've ever seen."

"Thank you."

Price laughed. "It's cute for another week. I'm having my apartment packed up and shipped out here. Then she'll have my stuff mixed with hers, again."

Fiona moved to him. "I can't wait."

Sadie moved around the room looking at the photos on the mantel and the walls. Fiona watched as she came to the newest collection—the ones she'd put up only two days ago.

Sadie turned to Fiona. "What are all the sonogram photos?"

Price's arm wrapped around Fiona's shoulders, and he pulled her in close.

"Those are our babies," Fiona said, and her voice hitched. "Every time we lost one, I put their picture in a box to forget. We decided, they were still our children, and they're waiting for us. So we're not hiding them in a box. They need to be celebrated."

Sadie's eyes went wide and immediately filled with tears. Charlie moved in next to her and pulled her to him.

"Fiona, I'm so sorry."

Fiona shook her head. "Don't be. It's part of who we are and how we got to this moment."

Leona reached a hand to Fiona and rested it on her arm. "I think it's precious."

Rosalyn wiped her fingers under her eyes, and Fiona knew she was transported back to those nights where she sat with Fiona after those losses while the men made music elsewhere.

"Let's eat," Price said. "We have some things planned after, and I'm a little anxious to get to them."

THEY HAD DINNER WITH THEIR FRIENDS AT THE DINING ROOM table, and Fiona's heart was full. That book she'd been working on, the one that wouldn't have the happily ever after, well, that was going to have to change. Because among those she had always loved, and the new friends she cherished with all her heart, she was happy—oh, so happy.

Price pushed back his chair from the table. "We have dessert. A cake." He took Fiona's hand and squeezed it. "A wedding cake. But first we need to have a wedding."

Price stood and walked to the other room and came back carrying a piece of paper.

"You're all here tonight to be part of our wedding."

Every woman at the table sucked in a breath and wiped tears from their cheeks. Every man nodded and smiled.

Fiona stood and kissed Price on the cheek. "We've written new vows that we'd like to share with each other, and then we want you all to sign the marriage license as witnesses. But write small. There are only two lines," she said, and everyone laughed.

Fiona retreated to the other room, just as Price had earlier, and she came back with her iPad.

"I needed a bigger copy to see," she teased as she opened it and faced Price.

"To Price. What once was, will never be. From here, I'll go it alone." She looked up at him and his brows had drawn together. She smiled. "When I moved here, I started a new book. In my heart, I knew it would be the first book I ever wrote that didn't have a happy ending. But, it was okay, because maybe I needed to believe that not everything ended happily. That was the dedication to the book. Interesting that it was dedicated to you."

Fiona brushed her finger over the screen and read aloud her amended dedication.

"To Price. Happily ever afters start with optimistic beginnings, even if those beginnings are second, third, or fourth ones. You will always be my happily ever after, and we will forever carry our family in our hearts—Chloe, Christian, Alexander, Leia, Sammi, and Benjamin."

She heard Sadie gasp, and then sob. Again, Charlie pulled her to him and held her.

"That was beautiful, Fiona," Sadie said softly.

Price nodded, moving in and kissing Fiona softly on the lips. "It was beautiful."

"The story changes now, Price. I'll never not want to love you again."

He smiled at her before kissing her again.

"Well, I'm not as good with the words. So, my vows have no words," he said as he moved to the piano in the living room. "This, my love, is for you."

Price sat down on the bench and stretched out his fingers. Then, as he lay his fingers on the keys, a melody she recognized played, only then did it turn. She closed her eyes and pictured colors and meadows. It was something she used to do when he'd write. His melodies were transforming, and she could see them in her mind.

He'd rewritten Fiona's Wedding Song, and this version had happy chords that made her head swim with bright light.

It was beautiful, absolutely beautiful.

When he finished, everyone at the table applauded, and Fiona opened her eyes.

"Colorful," she said, looking at Price.

"You are every melody that has ever stuck in my head, my love," he said as he rose and moved to her. "I know now, that being right here, right now, this is the good stuff."

PART III
HAPPILY EVER AFTER

CHAPTER 41

Leona pinched the bridge of her nose trying to ward off the headache that was starting as she stared at the computer screen.

She loved her business—everything about it even. But taxes made her consider closing the store and moving far away to a secluded island every single year.

Fiona poked her head through the door of the break room and Leona lifted her head from her computer.

"There's a man out here who needs to talk to you."

Leona lifted an eyebrow. "Tell me he's an accountant and he'd love to do taxes for free."

Fiona chuckled. "I don't think so. He's got on work boots."

Crinkling up her nose, Leona set her pencil down on the notepad she'd scribbled a million numbers on, and stood.

She followed Fiona out to the store, which even on a Monday morning, was bustling.

"Can I help you?" Leona approached the man, not only in work boots, but faded jeans with a rip near the pocket and a dangling belt loop. He had on a Carhartt T-shirt, and a pair of work gloves hung from his back pocket.

"Jon Ford," he said as if she'd asked his name. "We're doing some work on the residences upstairs and they're having some plumbing issues. We're shutting off the water to the entire building."

"Leona," she added her name as he had done, unsolicited as well. "How long will that be for?"

"No idea, ma'am," he said sternly, cocking his head to the side as he did so. "It'll be off until we're done."

Leona bit the inside of her cheek when Jon Ford called her ma'am. But it was his tone when he said, *until we're done,* that had heat rising beneath her skin.

"I don't see that I have a choice."

"Nope," This time he cocked his head to the other side. "Just wanted you to know."

"Do I need to do anything here in the store?" she asked.

"No. Guess you could fill some coffee pots or teacups," he said chewing a piece of gum he must have had tucked in his cheek.

Leona flared her nostrils. "We'll make sure to do that," Leona snapped. "You'll let us know when it's turned back on?"

"If I remember."

Leona drew in a breath. "Thank you, Mr. Ford."

He nodded, still chewing that gum. "Yup."

As he started for the door, it opened, and Sadie walked past him. She said hello, and Leona wondered if he just grunted in return.

"He's cute," Sadie said with a smile. "No, I'm not looking."

Fiona laughed and headed back to her desk in the corner to write.

Sadie studied Leona. "Are you okay? You don't look right."

Leona lifted her hand to scratch her head, only to find a pencil stuck in her hair. She let out a groan. "I'm fine. I've just been working on taxes and it's given me a headache."

"I could make you some tea," Sadie offered and the mention of it only intensified the headache.

"They're turning off our water. The residences upstairs are having plumbing problems."

Sadie nodded. "I could run down the street and get you a drink."

Leona looked out the front window of her store and noticed that a large pickup truck with the name *Ford Fix It* on the door.

The headache throbbed behind Leona's eyes and she pressed her fingers to her eyes.

"You know, I think I'll walk down there myself and get something. The walk and the sunshine will do me good." She turned and set the pencil she'd found in her hair, on the counter. "I'll bring you and Fiona something back."

"We'll hold down the fort," Sadie said as Leona pulled her small, beaded purse from under the counter and headed out the door.

JON STUDIED THE BOARD BEHIND THE COUNTER AT THE COFFEE shop. Why was it that places like this had to make up names for everything? He'd had to search to find out that a Dirty Joe, was a regular cup of strong coffee, though he'd ask for a regular coffee, like he did every time he'd been there.

Charlie lifted his head from behind the partition on the other side of the counter and smiled. "Hey, Jon," he said in that happy tone he seemed to always have. Jon envied that trait in the younger man. It certainly wasn't one that Jon possessed.

"Hey, Charlie. How's your grandmother?"

A smile formed on Charlie's mouth. "She remembered me this morning. It's a good day."

"That's good."

"Regular coffee?" Charlie asked and Jon was grateful to not have asked for a Dirty Joe.

"Yeah. Make it as big as they come."

Charlie nodded and took the money Jon fished from his pocket.

Jon moved to the end of the counter to wait.

"Hey, Leona," he heard Charlie's voice and Jon lifted his head to see the woman he'd just spoken to ordering drinks.

He scanned a look over her. Long flowing skirt, beaded necklaces that hung from her neck, and dangly earrings. She must have had thirty bracelets on her wrist and rings on most of her fingers.

From the color of her hair, with only a few strands of gray, and the lack of deep lines around her eyes—because he'd noticed —he figured they were close in age. His grandmother would say that the woman's soul was old.

She paid for her drinks and moved to the end of the counter next to him.

"Hey," he said drawing her attention to him.

There was no smile that came to her lips or lit in her eyes. Not that he expected anything different. He wasn't much of a people person.

"Hello, Mr. Ford."

She was polite, formal, and stiff.

His name was called and he reached for his drink. "See ya round, ma'am." He gave her a nod and strode off.

Taking his gum out of his mouth, he tossed it into the trash can, and sipped his coffee.

Another truck pulled up and parked behind his in front of the bookstore—the plumber. Finally, he could get started on the job at hand. But that building was old, and he was afraid before they had it fixed, there would be more problems.

CHAPTER 42

LEONA WATCHED *FORD FIX IT* WALK DOWN THE STREET, AND SHE shook her head. Sadie had been right, he was cute. But what was it about a man like that who used few words and could still infuriate someone?

Then again, she wondered, was it the inconvenience that the toilet and sink wouldn't work for a while? Maybe it was that he called her ma'am or told her that the job would be done when they finished it, or maybe it was just the taxes.

Charlie moved to the end of the counter, tray of coffees in his hand. "Here you go."

Leona moved toward him to take the tray and noticed that there was a bag in the open section of the tray.

He was smiling when she looked up at him. "Sadie says you're doing taxes. There's two big cookies in there for you to enjoy while you're crunching numbers. It always helps me when I'm working on a paper for school."

"I appreciate that, Charlie."

"My pleasure," he said, smiling, and Leona was sure it had been his pleasure. It was just the kind of man he was. Sadie was a lucky girl.

Leona's mood was slightly more elevated than it had been, and when the man walking in the door to the store held it open for her, she thought that there was some hope for humanity.

Leona set the coffees on the counter and looked around to find Sadie, hip propped up against Fiona's desk. She had Fiona's laptop in her hand and was reading.

Leona picked up the two coffees she'd bought for the women and walked toward them.

She handed Fiona her drink and waited for Sadie to finish reading whatever she was reading.

Tears had pooled in Sadie's eyes, and Fiona looked up at her with an enormous grin.

When Sadie was done, she drew in an unsteady breath and handed Fiona her laptop and then wiped her eyes.

"That was beautiful. I mean," she blew out a breath and held her hand to her chest, "wow."

Leona handed Sadie her coffee.

"Is that part of your new book?" Leona asked Fiona.

"Yes. Not the one I started before, but this is a new one." She sighed. "Since Price and I got married again, the words just keep coming. For him too, with his music. I have to be here to write because he's writing music like crazy."

"I thought he wasn't going to write anymore."

Fiona shook her head. "He's not going to tour. But I told him he should record his new stuff. It's amazing."

Leona smiled as she turned back to the counter and her coffee. Behind her, she could hear the other two women talking about the men they loved and cherished.

Looking out the window at her obscured view, Leona sipped her coffee. She was happy for her friends, and she was proud to have had a little part in the coming together of those couples. From switching the books that Charlie and Sadie had bought, to making sure Price was at the book signing for Fiona, and at the end of the line so he could have more time to talk to her.

Leona believed in happily ever afters. So much so, she named her store after it. But, the truth was, she'd never had her own.

Well, that wasn't true. Her store was her entire life. She was obsessed with making it the best store in town. The lines at signings were proof to her that she did her job well.

But having a man by her side, who loved her like Charlie and Price loved Sadie and Fiona, that eluded her.

Sipping her coffee, she watched as Jon, the fix it guy, walked to his truck. With one hand, he held his cell phone to his ear, and with the other, he gestured as if the person on the other end would understand him better. He was pointing up at the building, then waving his hand back and forth, before he dragged his fingers through the dark wavy hair atop his head.

It was when Leona realized that detail that she picked up her cookie bag and coffee, and headed back to finish those dreaded taxes.

"THE PIPES ARE SHOT," JON SHOUTED INTO THE PHONE AT THE owner of the building. "This isn't a repair job. If you don't have the pipes replaced, you're going to have a lot of trouble."

Jon listened to the incompetent owner of the building tell him how he didn't feel there was a need to put money into a building where everyone was happy being there.

"That might be the case, sir, but if one of those pipes goes, it could flood the apartments as well as the businesses below. You have an antique store and a bookstore full of inventory at risk."

Those facts didn't seem to matter to the man. Jon was sent to repair the crack they had found and to be on his way.

Jon disconnected the call, tucked his phone into his pocket, and pressed his fingers to his eyes.

When he'd walked through the antique store and the bookstore, he'd taken the time to look at their ceilings and walls, which were mostly covered with shelves of inventory. Though the weathered look gave the right atmosphere to the stores, he wondered just how dilapidated the building really was.

Jon blew out a breath and headed back upstairs to discuss the situation with the plumber that had come to do the technical stuff.

When owners of buildings hindered him from doing his job, but hired him, it reflected badly on his business when things went wrong anyway. The problem was, he didn't have a choice. He needed the work. Ballet lessons didn't pay for themselves, neither did tee-ball, school lunches, or health insurance. He had plenty saved away, but rainy days came more often than opportunity. If he could buy the building, he would.

As he walked into the building, he took his phone from his pocket and called his mother.

When he'd explained his situation, he leaned against the wall in the hallway before entering the apartment.

"We'll take care of them, honey. We are your village," she said cheerfully.

"I appreciate it, Mom."

"You know we're always here for you."

Jon ran his tongue over his teeth and tightly closed his eyes for a moment. Yes, he knew his parents would be there for anything he needed. He just wished they didn't have to be.

CHAPTER 43

Fiona had offered to stay and close the store so that Leona could go home and get some rest. Obviously, her day in the back room hovering over numbers had made her something of a grouch.

She'd refused the offer and sent Fiona on her way. Now, at eight-thirty, she sat in the dark of her store, behind the counter, and sipped at a Pepsi she'd found in the back of the little refrigerator. The water was still off, and she wanted to make sure she was around when they turned it back on.

It was only supposed to be off for a little while, yet there she was waiting.

Jon Ford's truck, which she noted was a Chevy, was still parked out front, and the plumber's truck was parked behind it. His day, too, must not have gone as planned.

She took another sip of her Pepsi, and noticed the plumber's truck pulling away from the curb. A moment later, she watched as Jon Ford cupped his hands around his eyes and peered into her store.

It was about time.

Leona moved to the door. He was standing there when she opened it, and it gave her heart a little start. She hadn't seen him move from the window.

"I didn't mean to startle you," he said, his voice deep and tired.

"It's okay. I'd seen you looking in. Water is back on?"

He ran his hand over the back of his neck. "For now. Would you mind if I came in and looked around though? I just want to make sure that nothing got through their floor."

Leona swallowed hard. "Is that a possibility?"

"I don't think so. But I don't half-do jobs. I'd like to just make sure."

He looked weary, and Leona wasn't sure why that tugged at her heart as it had. As long as he didn't call her ma'am, she didn't see any problem with letting him in.

Leona watched as he walked through the store, starting on the perimeter and looking up. Every so often, he'd stop with his flashlight.

She walked to the break room and found a plastic red cup on the shelf by the coffee pot. When she looked at the table where she'd worked all day, there was the bag with the cookies in it. She hadn't even touched them.

She picked up the bag and went back to the counter.

Jon looked at every corner, and a few times, touched the wall with his hand. Leona watched him walk into the back room and turned on the light. She heard the water running in the small sink, and then it turned off.

Next, he went into the bathroom. The light turned on. The sink turned on, then off. Then the toilet flushed.

Jon turned off the light as he walked out to the store area.

"Everything good?" she asked, pouring some Pepsi into the red cup.

"It looks alright," he said, but there was something in how he said it that didn't give her a lot of peace.

She held out the cup. "You look like you could use a little something. It's just Pepsi. It's not laced or anything."

Jon took the cup. "Thank you."

"You look like you had a rough day. Would you like to sit for a moment? I have two cookies."

He raised a brow, and she knew she sounded desperate. Maybe she was. For some reason, she just didn't want to be alone at that moment.

JON SIPPED THE PEPSI AND CONTEMPLATED THE OFFER. IT HAD gotten late enough that his mother asked him to leave the kids with her. They, of course, were ecstatic, but guilt swam in his gut over it.

Leona motioned to the stool next to her, and he decided to take it. His feet and back ached. A few moments off them would be delightful.

"Thanks."

She smiled, and in the shadows, he was sure he'd even seen her eyes sparkle when she did so. Her eyes certainly hadn't done that when he'd met her that morning.

Leona picked up the bag and withdrew the two enormous cookies. Jon couldn't help but smile when she handed him one.

"These are my downfall," he admitted as he took a bite.

Leona bit into hers and he heard her moan. "I don't think I ate today," she said. "The sugar in the cookie and the Pepsi should have me up all night. Maybe I should have waited to do my taxes until midnight."

Jon snorted a laugh and that made Leona smile.

"I didn't eat today either," he said as he bit into his cookie. "My evening plans got changed because of how long all of this took today. You wouldn't be interested in going and getting something to eat, would you?"

Her eyes went wide and the smile disappeared.

Jon shook his head. "I'm sorry. I don't know where that came from. You probably needed to get home to your husband, and me asking you to dinner was inappropriate."

Leona bit down on her lip and then lifted her cup to take a sip of her drink. "I'm not married," she said.

"Oh. Still, I should have asked first."

"The pizza place is open until eleven."

"Best slices of pepperoni in town."

Leona wrinkled her nose. "Mushroom and onion."

"That's all you put on pizza?" He bit into his cookie and spoke with his mouth full, "That's not a pizza."

"It sure is," she said standing, and her bracelets clanked together. "I'll give you a bite, and you'll find out."

Jon watched her stand and take her jacket from the hook behind her. There was something wildly exciting about a woman who got that worked up over a slice of pizza.

Jon took the two halves of the two cookies that were left and slid them back into the bag from the coffee shop. She eyed him as she turned around.

"We'll leave these for tomorrow," he said.

"You'll be back tomorrow?"

He nodded. "I want to check up on the job and make sure everything is just right."

She stared at him thoughtfully. "I didn't think fix-it men did that kind of thing."

"Ensure that the job was done right?"

Her brow furrowed. "Yep." She blew out a breath. "And I'm tired and hangry. I apologize for that. That was uncalled for."

"I'm more than used to it," he admitted.

"No matter. It shouldn't have come from me." She slipped on her jacket. "If you're not inclined to hightail it out of here, I'll buy you a slice of pepperoni pizza."

Now he smiled. "I'll take you up on it, as long as you don't make me taste yours."

"We'll see," she said as she started for the door with him in tow.

CHAPTER 44

CRISP APRIL AIR STIRRED AS THEY WALKED DOWN THE STREET, their hands in their pockets. They walked in silence, but Leona didn't feel as if it were an awkward silence.

When they reached the restaurant, Jon pulled open the door and Leona stepped through.

"Thank you."

"My pleasure," he said.

They walked around the wall and looked up at the menu. A young woman came to the register. "Hey, Leona," the girl said. Then she adjusted her glance. "Hi, Mr. Ford."

Leona shifted a look toward him before she looked back at the girl. "Hello, Amber. A slice with mushroom and onion. And," she hummed, "an unsweetened iced tea."

"You got it." Amber lifted her eyes from the register up to Jon. "And a pepp for you?"

He smiled. "Yes."

"Do you want a beer?"

He shook his head, but Leona wondered why.

She lifted her finger. "You know, I'll take a beer. Michelob Light."

Amber nodded and looked back at Jon.

He grinned. "Why not. But make mine Bud. Full strength."

Amber gave them the total and before Leona could whip out her credit card, Jon had handed over the cash.

"I don't think that was the deal," Leona whispered.

"You shared your cookie stash. It's fair."

As Amber handed him back his change, she smiled at him. "I'm free on Saturday night if you want me," she said, and Jon chewed his lip as he put the money in his pocket.

"You're sure?"

Amber nodded.

"Okay. Five o'clock work?"

"Sure does. I'll be at your house then."

Amber gave them a little wave and moved on to the next customers in line.

As they moved down the corridor toward the pickup window, Leona replayed the conversation between Jon and Amber in her head.

The girl had been coming into her store for the better part of ten years, so Leona knew, though the girl was of legal age, she wasn't more than nineteen.

Jon on the other hand, well, he might have been younger than she was by a few years, but not many. What exactly did he have with a young college girl?

Maybe the fix-it guy rap wasn't any different from she thought after all. Sleazy guys who fix stuff, run off when the job goes badly, and they have a thing for much too young blondes.

It broke her heart. She thought so much more of Amber than that.

When their plates with the slices of pizza, which took up the entire plate, and their bottles of beer were slid toward them, they each moved in, bumping shoulders.

"Sorry," he said as he eased back and let Leona in. "Guess I'm hungry."

She didn't respond. The entire exchange with Amber had Leona seething. Especially since Amber had called him Mr. Ford, and not Jon.

Leona chose a table right in the middle of the restaurant to sit. There weren't many people there at nine o'clock on a Monday night, but a few.

As soon as she sat, she began to bite into her slice.

Jon eased his plate to the table, and then his bottle. Shrugging out of his coat, he hung it on the back of his chair and then sat down.

"Are you in a hurry? You didn't even take off your coat," he said, lifting his beer to his lips and taking a sip.

"I don't want to keep you out for long."

"I'm a grown man. I haven't asked for permission to stay out late in a long time. But, in fact, before I went into your store, I happened to have talked to my mother, and she gave me permission."

Leona wasn't sure what to do with that. So she jumped into the argument that tightened her chest. "So you know Amber?" She asked, and the words were sharp.

Jon nodded as he lifted his slice to his mouth and took a bite. "Sure. She's lived here all her life. So have I. I graduated with her father, who, by the way, is still a good friend."

"She comes to your house?"

Leona saw his jaw tense as he took a long pull from his beer.

Jon's eyes went dark, and she was quite sure she'd over-stepped some boundary.

"I noticed she called you by your first name," he said, taking a bite of his slice. "You must be pretty chummy for her to do that."

Leona wasn't sure what the young woman would do at his house, but he was right. She'd called Leona by her name, and she'd referred to Jon as Mr. Ford.

"She's been a customer since she was a young girl."

Jon nodded his head. "I've known her since she was born. You might find it interesting to know I attended her first birthday party. It was a Dora the Explorer party."

Leona sipped her beer, and it burned in her chest. "I'm sorry. I didn't mean to..."

"Accuse me of something you know nothing about?"

And the curt side of him that had originally put her into a mood that morning was back. So the gentle side of him eating cookies and drinking Pepsi was short-lived between moods.

Perhaps she deserved this mood. She had been accusatory.

Leona picked up her pizza and focused on getting it eaten and her beer drank. She couldn't down her beer as he had, but she was sure he would sit there until Leona was done.

"I'm going to get another beer," Jon said. "Would you like one?"

That very statement puzzled her. If he had one more beer, they'd have to sit there and spend a few more moments together. Certainly he wouldn't want to do that.

"No," she said. "I'm fine."

He nodded, stood, and walked toward the counter where Amber took his order. They exchanged friendly banter, and Leona felt small. He never did tell her why Amber would arrive at his house at five on Saturday, but for a man who had only introduced himself that morning, she supposed she had no right to assume he'd answer anyway.

When he returned, he sat down with his beer and finished his pizza.

By the time Leona had finished her slice and her beer, Jon had finished his second beer.

They stood, threw away their trash, and started their walk back to the bookstore.

"What time do you arrive in the mornings?" Jon asked as they neared the store.

"Eight."

"I'll stop in tomorrow to make sure everything is good

upstairs, and still good in your store. And then, you'll be done with me."

Leona nodded as she fished her keys from her pocket and unlocked the door of the store. "Thank you for dinner. That was very kind of you."

Jon opened the passenger door of his truck, shrugged out of his jacket, and threw it into the cab.

"It definitely beat a cold Pop Tart over the sink."

He stood at his truck as if he'd dropped her off from a date and waited for her to go inside.

"I'll see you tomorrow then."

Just as she stepped into the store, he called to her. "Do you park out back?"

"Yes."

"I'll wait by the alley just to make sure you get going safely."

"Oh you don't have—"

"That same mother that gave me permission to stay out later tonight would be less than impressed if I didn't make sure your car started, and you were safe."

Leona nodded. "I won't be but a minute," she said as she closed and locked the door to the store.

Through the window, she watched him look up at the star drenched sky, run his fingers through his hair, and then climb into his truck and start it.

As she gathered her bags and items for home, Leona thought her day had certainly been filled with the unexpected.

CHAPTER 45

Jon tapped on the front door. The porch light flicked on, and his mother opened the door, standing in the dark house in her robe.

"You didn't have to come over. I told you they're fine," she whispered as Jon stepped into the house.

"I know. I brought their bags with clothes for daycare tomorrow. I figured I'd just sleep on the couch."

His mother reached up to his hair and soothed her hand over it. "Jon, you have to let go. They're okay to be away from you for the night."

He nodded. "Maybe I'm not okay."

She took the bags from him and put them by the door. "C'mon, let's get you some pillows and a blanket."

Jon followed his mother through the house he'd grown up in. She maneuvered through the dark and collected the items.

"Go kiss them," she said as she headed back to the couch to make it up for him.

Jon went to the bedroom where his son and daughter slept in the same bed. Each of them held tightly to an item that gave them comfort. Sean held his quilt, which was now nothing more than a few pieces of fabric stitched together. His tiny thumb was in his mouth, and he was pressed up next to his sister.

Jon lifted the comforter to cover Sean's little body. He pressed a kiss to his head, taking a moment to smell his sweetness.

Walking around to the other side of the bed, Jon brushed back Penny's hair and kissed her forehead. She shifted and wrapped her arms tightly around the doll that had been her mother's.

Jon looked down at the two people who were his entire world. His heart squeezed in his chest.

"It's ready," his mother's voice whispered from the doorway.

Jon nodded and moved to her. "Am I doing okay by them?"

His mother rested her hand on his arm. "Yes, honey. They're doing wonderful. So some days you work late. Dad and I love having them. We're always here to help you."

"I just feel as if they need more than just me."

She shook her head. "They have us and each other too. Sweetheart, let's let them sleep."

Jon and his mother turned from the bedroom and walked back to the living room.

"Do you want some tea?" his mother asked, and Jon winced.

"No. I'll just get to sleep."

His mother lifted on her toes and kissed his cheek. "Okay. I love you."

She went back to her room and Jon settled down on the couch.

He was grateful for his parents, especially his poor mother who had spent the past three years listening to him worry about being a good enough parent.

He worried that he wasn't enough for them, a single dad who sometimes worked too much. She always assured him that they were well taken care of, both physically and monetarily.

There were times he thought it was stupid to worry about someone else's shoddy plumbing.

But, what if it weren't someone else's building? What if Jon bought the building? He could fix it, tear it down and rebuild it, or remodel it. Then he could keep it nice for the tenants who would pay him to run their businesses and live in the building.

Instead, he took jobs fixing plumbing, repairing floors, and painting walls to make sure that his children would have everything they ever needed, especially since they didn't have their mother with them.

Jon sat down on the couch and pulled off his work boots and socks. He noticed a pair of his father's pajama bottoms draped over the arm of the couch, and he chuckled. His mother would think about everything.

He slipped on the pajama pants, pounded the pillow his mother had left for him and then lay back on the couch. He tucked his hands under his head and let out a cleansing breath.

Then, his mind went to Leona. He wasn't sure what had made him ask her to dinner, though that had been a disaster. She was standoffish and that had come across loud and clear from the moment he'd walked into her store.

Then again, he hadn't been the most charming when he'd met her that morning.

Jon had done work on that building for years. It surprised him that he'd never been into the bookstore. Of course, he was still sure that the pipes in the building were going to need to be replaced, and that would mean he'd be in the store more often.

His wife had loved the bookstore, which could have been why Jon had never stepped into it.

She'd read every romance novel she could get her hands on, and he'd tease her that he'd never live up to those kinds of men. But in her honest and loving way, she'd always assure him that he was exactly the romance she'd wanted.

What would she think of him now? He'd aged in three years and grown more cynical and angry.

What did Leona think of him?

He rolled to his side, pounding the pillow again.

Jon wanted her to enjoy his company, though he wasn't sure why it was important. He'd only met her, but there was a need for her to like him. Hell, a woman who would share her chocolate chip cookie had to be attracted to a man, right?

The thought humored him. Was he so desperate to feel again that he'd lose sleep over a woman he'd just met?

He chuckled.

It wasn't that, he thought. There was something about Leona that had made him feel alive for the first time in years. And that feeling had zipped right through him before he'd even spoke to her. It was the feeling he got walking into her crowded, eclectic store. It was hearing the bracelets on her arm, seeing the specks of gray that mixed into her wild curls, and the warmth of her voice, even though she was hard at first.

They'd eased around each other quickly. Dinner should have been a delight, but her assumptions over Amber had him seething.

He covered his eyes with his arm. When she'd asked—or accused—he hadn't given her a reason to understand the situation. Not once had he mentioned his family.

Tomorrow, he thought as he closed his eyes. He'd see how things panned out tomorrow. Maybe Leona would be open to going for coffee and finishing those chocolate chip cookies.

Jon chuckled to himself again.

After all of that, maybe he'd call the owner of that building and see how much he'd take to surrender ownership. Perhaps owning a building and collecting rents would allow him time with his family. And then, fixing the plumbing for the tenants wouldn't be such a big deal.

CHAPTER 46

Before Leona even walked into the main part of her store, she brewed a cup of tea, eyed the two half-eaten cookies, and then checked the temperature. April still carried coolness in the morning, but the store seemed chillier than normal.

The thermostat was set to sixty-five, and would usually be adjusted throughout the day depending on the number of people in the store. Today, though, the furnace hadn't kicked on to keep the temperature current, and it was reading fifty-nine.

She carried her mug to the front counter and noticed the *Ford Fix It* truck out front. So, Jon Ford was a man of his word. He said he'd come by and he had.

Though she felt bad for the comment about fix-it people in general, she'd found that statement to be more than true. When something was fixed, it was usually never checked on after.

Perhaps she could convince him to look into the furnace while he was there.

The moment she sat down at the front counter to check her emails, she noticed Jon climb from his truck and head toward her store.

She stood and crossed to the front door, unlocking it as he approached.

"I didn't actually expect to see you so early," she said as she opened the door.

"Yeah, I'm waiting on the plumber. There's more work to do upstairs than the owner let us tend to yesterday."

Leona stepped back so Jon could walk in. "He's a cheapskate. Bare minimum."

Jon growled. "Yeah. But he thinks I'm screwing with him when I make suggestions. So what do you do?"

Leona frowned. "I've often thought of buying the whole building," she said and heat rose up her neck because the conversation had been had many times. "Then I could renovate it the way I'd like to."

She watched Jon's eyes flash dark, but then the corner of his mouth curled up.

"What?" she asked.

"I thought the same thing last night. It kept me awake. Well, that and sleeping on my mother's couch."

"You slept on your mother's couch? What's wrong with your house?"

He chewed his bottom lip. "Nothing." He looked around the dark and quiet store. "It's cold in here."

Leona blinked hard. "Yes. I was going to ask you about that. Would you look at the furnace? It's set to sixty-five, but it says it's fifty-nine in here."

Jon nodded. "I'd be happy to. You got coffee in the back?"

Leona nodded. "I'll make you some."

"I'd appreciate it."

Leona walked to the back room and Jon followed.

As he looked at the furnace, she brewed a single cup of coffee for him, and then stood with her back pressed to the doorjamb and watched him.

"Your pilot light is out. Give me ten minutes, and I'll have you up and running," he said as he stood and moved toward the door to pass her.

She didn't move to allow him the space, and she wasn't sure why.

There was something about the broody, dark, and handsome stranger that ignited something deep inside her.

"Can I get through?" he asked, his voice low as he stood right in front of her smelling of nothing but soap.

"Sorry," she managed as she stepped out of the way.

By the time he'd returned from his truck, she had his coffee on the small table in the center of the room, along with the other half of his cookie. Leona nibbled on her cookie and sipped on her tea.

"Nothing better than cookies for breakfast," Jon teased as he walked to the furnace and knelt down in front of it.

"I didn't want you to forget it was here."

"Oh, I didn't forget," he said as he pushed a button on the furnace and flicked the lighter in his hand.

Leona held her breath as he lit the pilot light. It always made her nervous to see that happen, and yet nothing ever went wrong.

"You're all set," Jon said.

"I appreciate it. The girls will too."

"My pleasure." He rose to his feet and then moved to pick up the coffee mug that waited for him.

"Let me know what I owe you."

He watched her over the top of his coffee mug. "When do you close on Saturday?"

Leona narrowed her eyes on him. "Five-thirty."

He nodded slowly to her response.

"Why?"

"Dinner?"

Her chest tightened and there was a flutter in her belly, but then she thought about the dinner they'd had the night before.

"Don't you already have plans?" she asked as he picked up his cookie and took a bite.

He chewed slowly. "I didn't say I had plans."

"You have plans with Amber."

Jon ran his tongue over his teeth, then sipped his coffee. "If that's what you think—"

"I'm wrong?"

"You're wrong," he said. "But I'll let you think on it." He picked up his cookie. "Can I bring back the mug?"

Leona nodded.

"Thanks. I'll catch ya later then," Jon said as he moved by her and out of the store.

Leona watched as he stood outside the building drinking the coffee from her mug, and looking up at the building. She couldn't help but wonder if he really saw the potential in the building, just as she did.

When the plumbing truck pulled up behind his truck, Jon opened the passenger door, put the mug on the dashboard, and walked upstairs with the plumber in tow.

CHAPTER 47

THINGS WERE NOT GOOD. THE FIXES THAT THEY'D MADE TO THE pipes in the apartment over the bookstore were solid fixes. Unfortunately, manipulation of the pipes to fix the original leak had caused more leaks.

Jon fumed as he tried to discuss the situation with the owner of the building, who wouldn't even meet them, but would only talk to Jon on the phone.

They'd had to turn the water off for the entire building, and now he had to let every tenant know, again, that they'd be without water. What was it about people who owned buildings thinking that collecting rents was all there was to it?

He left the plumber to fix the new leaks, and made his way to every tenant, meeting Leona in the very narrow stairwell to the second floor.

"I was just coming down to see you," he said as they stood nearly toe to toe on the stairs looking at one another.

"To tell me I'll be without water again?"

Jon bit the inside of his cheek to calm himself from the bite of her comment. "Yep."

"What is going on? The pipes in my store are rattling more than normal."

"Well, we have a bigger problem than normal."

"Can you fix it?" she snapped the question as she folded her arms in front of her.

Jon mimicked her stance. "I can fix it. But I can only do as much as that owner will foot the bill for. This entire building is old enough that everything needs to be rerun, or it's just going to keep breaking. And it's going to break, and leak, into every unit in this building. Including yours."

Her face contorted into something between irritation and anger. "And you've told him all of this, in detail?"

"Of course I have. Do you want to call him? Maybe you can be more persuasive."

"I'll do better than that," she bit out. "I'll go talk to him in person."

"I'm right behind you, doll. Let's make this happen."

She spun to face him. Now they were nose to nose, and her eyes lit angry, but the small twitch of her mouth made Jon stir inside, like he hadn't in years.

"Don't call me doll."

"No problem," he countered.

"You don't have to go with me."

Jon shrugged. "I have some words."

Leona's brow furrowed. "He's not a very nice man."

"I've spoken to him," Jon admitted. "I know that first-hand."

"I can handle this."

Leona turned to walk away, but Jon reached for her, took hold of her hand and stopped her.

They both looked down to where their hands joined, but he didn't let go.

"You shouldn't have to do this alone. Or at all. I was hired to do a job, and my reputation is on the line if this all goes badly. I can handle it."

Leona worried her lip. "Trust me on this one."

"Then just let me go with you. I'll drive."

She shook her head. "I'm not riding in your work truck."

"What's wrong with my work truck?"

"If we go, I'll drive," she countered. and Jon decided he had no choice if he wanted to confront the man.

"Fine."

LEONA MADE CALLS TO SADIE AND FIONA, ASKING THEM TO OPEN the store. She didn't give them any other information, and they didn't ask.

Jon followed her through the store and out the back door to her car. She hit the fob to unlock the doors, and then climbed in behind the driver's seat.

"You're kidding me with this?" Jon asked, as he did everything he could to slide into the Mini-Cooper with his long legs and tall torso. "If you crash, they'll never extract me from this thing."

"I'm not going to crash," she defended herself.

"Yeah, and I'm never going to get my legs to unfold," he grunted as he managed into the car. "My truck is clean."

Leona let out a breath. "Sorry. I just need an ounce of control in this situation."

She started the car and backed out of the parking space. Driving down the alley, she slowed when she came to the street. Taking a moment to calm herself, she didn't pull onto the street.

"You know where you're going?" Jon asked.

"Do you?"

He shook his head. "Nope."

Resigned, Leona nodded. "Yes. I know."

"He's this bad? I mean you're out of sorts."

Leona pulled onto the street and drove. "You've known me less than two days. You don't know my sorts."

There was a curl on his pursed lips, and she wondered if he

did know her. Had she met him? She thought she would have remembered him. Surely he wasn't a reader. He had rough, calloused hands, and always had a little stubble of a beard. If she had to guess, he worked from sunup to sundown to make the bills, and he fell into a recliner at the end of the day and put his feet up in front of the TV.

"So, you didn't answer my question," Jon said. "The owner of the building?"

Leona gripped her steering wheel tighter. "He's just had a hard life, and it settled into his personality."

"So you know him? I mean personally?"

"Yeah," she said. "I know him."

"How long have you been in business?"

"Twenty years."

Jon ran the back of his hand over the whiskers on his chin, and it scratched against his skin. "I wouldn't have pegged you to be much older than me. That means you're either older than I think, or you started your business very young."

"And how old do you think I am?" Leona asked as she flicked on her turn signal and turned down the next street.

"Oh, no. I'm not going there. I'll tell you that I'm thirty-eight, and I think you're close to that."

The smile that formed on her mouth couldn't be helped. "I'm not much older."

"Are you going to tell me?"

She pursed her lips. "Let's just say when young *Ford Fix It* was born, I was learning my A-B-C's in kindergarten."

He nodded slowly. "So you were young when you opened your store," he commented, and she knew he'd done the math.

"An opportunity arose and I took it."

"Pretty impressive."

She shifted a glance at him. "How old were you when you started your business?"

He ran his tongue over his teeth. "Not as young."

"Okay, how many years ago?"

Jon chuckled. "Eight."

Leona grinned, having done the math. "Still young."

"Yeah, that's what a lot of the old guys who own buildings around here said too, when I approached them to sell their properties. Headstrong community."

"You want to buy buildings?"

"As many as I can. And then, I'll fix those, and I won't have to worry about little side jobs."

Leona understood that statement more than she cared to. Not only the owning, but the lack of respect when someone young wanted to do big things.

CHAPTER 48

LEONA PULLED INTO THE PARKING LOT OF THE CARE FACILITY AND parked the car. Jon looked around as Leona opened her door and began to climb out of the little car with ease.

"What are we doing here?" he asked as he managed to open his door.

"We're meeting with the owner of the building," she said as he tried to unfold his legs out the door and then manage his shoulders out without smacking his head.

"He has an office here?"

She laughed. "No."

Hiking her purse up on her shoulder, she walked ahead of him. Her long skirt swayed, as did her curls. Every time she adjusted her purse strap, the bangles on her wrists chimed together.

It was a sight, Jon thought, as they walked toward the front doors.

When they entered, Leona turned to the right and Jon looked left. There was a small tingle at the base of his neck that said before they left, he should go to the other wing and drop in. But the other wing was memory care, and it broke his heart when he walked into a room and someone he cared about didn't know him. It had kept him away—perhaps for too long.

"Are you coming?" Leona had stopped and turned back to him.

"Yeah. Sorry."

He caught up to her as she turned into a community TV room and walked to a man seated by the window.

"Hey," she said softly, and the man turned to her.

He was dressed in a button-down shirt with a tie. His hair was neatly combed, and he didn't look as old as the rest of the residents in the room. He had his cell phone atop a notebook resting on his lap in his wheelchair.

"How are you today?" Leona asked as she pulled a chair up next to him and sat down.

"I'm good, honey. Just doing business."

Leona nodded and then looked up at Jon. "This is Jon Ford."

The man shot out his hand and Jon shook it.

"It's nice to meet you," Jon said, though he wasn't sure who he was meeting.

The man's face contorted, and his eyes narrowed. "The guy fixing the plumbing?"

Ah, okay, now he knew who he was. "Yes, sir."

"The man who wants me to spend all my money," the man said, and Leona rested a hand on his arm.

"Daddy, the building is in bad shape," Leona said, and Jon thought his legs just might give out. "You need to consider..."

"Sir, I'd like to buy the building from you," Jon said, and the man and Leona both looked up at him. "The building is in a prime location, but it's already a century old, and the plumbing and electrical are equally old."

Leona's eyes went wide, and her father shook his head. "Everyone wants to make a buck off of me," he scowled up at Jon.

"I'll give you a fair price. In fact, I'll even go above it. It's an amazing property, sir."

"Jon, stop," Leona instructed.

"Let him talk," her father said. "Oh, I can come up with a doozy of a price."

"Fair market, sir. I'm not looking to screw you or anyone else, and I'm not looking to get screwed either. I'm looking for an opportunity. If we don't get in there and replace the pipes in that building, it's going to be an unsafe place for people to live. And if those pipes go, the antique store and Leona's bookstore could be ruined."

Her eyes went wide as they looked up at him. "Seriously?"

Jon nodded. "I have the time, money, and know-how to fix it."

Leona's father bore a stare at her. "You stay," he said, and then turned his furrowed look at Jon. "You go."

"Daddy, I drove him—"

Jon held up a hand. "It's okay," he said as calmly as he could. "I'm going to go to the other wing and pay a visit to someone."

Leona nodded as Jon turned and walked away.

"You're very rude," Leona said as she sat back and crossed her arms in front of her.

"You brought him here to poke at me? To get me to fix the building?"

"No. He just tagged along. I came here to ask you to sell me the building."

Her father cackled. "A bidding war," his eyes went wide as he said it.

"You'd do that?"

"You make plenty of money." Her father picked up his notebook and opened it.

Leona looked down at it, but she couldn't read anything he'd written in it.

"You never appreciated the building before," he said to her, and it sliced right into her chest.

"Daddy, if you could only see what I've done there."

"How can I see it when I'm here?"

AND THAT WAS THE CARD HE'D DEALT HER. SHE'D PUT HIM IN A nursing home because he couldn't be taken care of at home. His mind was sharp, but his body had long ago been riddled with too many diseases, and she couldn't take care of him alone.

Her father ripped the piece of paper from his book and handed it to her. "This is how much I want for it. Tell him he has a week to respond and come up with it if he wants it."

"Daddy, let's just fix the building. You don't have to sell it."

"Why? Because if I sell it, you won't just get it in the end?"

Her heart broke. She'd never thought that way.

"Because it meant something to you once."

"Nothing in my life means anything to me anymore," he said, and Leona could feel the tears rise in her throat and sting her eyes.

"Daddy, I'm sorry."

"Go. Only come back if he has the money."

Leona nodded and stood. As she leaned in to kiss her father's cheek, he pulled back.

Not much had changed in the past ten years that he'd lived in the facility. He'd grown angrier and meaner.

Leona swore she'd never be that bitter, but the older she got, she wasn't sure it wouldn't happen. After all, at the end of the day, she was a forty-three-year-old woman with no husband, no children, and only a hateful old man in her life.

CHAPTER 49

⁂

Jon felt lost as he wandered down the halls of the care facility. There was a feeling of betrayal that ran through him, though he wasn't sure why. Leona hadn't owed him the knowledge that her father owned the building, but had he known, could have been a little gentler when he spoke to her about the horrible man that owned the building.

He wasn't even sure why he cared about the building at all. It wasn't as if he had anything personal to do with it, but he'd wanted it for as long as he could remember. And maybe that all circled back to his wife and the joy that the bookstore and antique store had brought to her.

Jon walked down the corridor and stopped outside the room he'd been looking for. The nameplate read Ellen McGowan.

Jon looked through the small window and saw her sitting by the window looking out. His heart pounded, but he felt as if a gentle hand had been placed on his shoulder. When Ellen looked up from the window and toward the door, he knew he had to go inside.

Pushing open the door, Jon noticed Charlie sitting in a chair across from Ellen.

"Hey," Jon said as he walked in.

Charlie's eyes lifted to him, but they held some kind of sadness, and Jon was sure it meant that it wasn't one of Ellen's better days. "Hey."

Ellen looked up at Jon and studied him. There was no earthly reason Ellen should know him. All he was going to do was confuse her. He should just say hello and go, but…

"Jon, sweetheart," Ellen said and both he and Charlie turned to look at her, holding her hand out to him. "Where are the kiddos?"

Jon swallowed hard and exchanged a look with Charlie, who shrugged.

"They're at daycare," he said kneeling down in front of her and taking the hand she offered. "They're getting big."

"I want to see."

Jon pulled his phone from his pocket and scrolled to the last picture he had of them. Sean wore his tee-ball shirt and had on his batting hat, and he leaned on his bat with one hand. Penny wore her unicorn dress with a multi-colored skirt and a unicorn on the front. They both smiled up at him as he turned the phone toward Ellen.

"Oh, aren't they precious." She looked up at him and then at Charlie. "Hello, Charlie," she said, and Charlie's eyes went wide and then soft.

"Hello, Grandma," he said, and smiled with the slightest shake of his head.

Ellen looked back down at the phone. "Where is Stacy?"

Jon tensed his jaw. What was he supposed to tell her? Should he lie? Was he supposed to tell the truth? He swallowed hard.

"Grandma, Stacy works long hours, remember?" Charlie said as he exchanged pained glances with Jon.

"You tell her to come see her grandma," Ellen said.

"I'll do that," Jon agreed, even though it ached in his chest to say it. He tucked his phone back in his pocket. "I was just in the area and thought I'd come say hello. You're looking well."

"I can't remember anything," Ellen laughed. "But my Charlie is waiting for me, and each day I get closer to being with him."

Jon's palms grew damp. Yeah, he understood that.

When the nurse walked in the door, Charlie stood and Jon rose.

"I need to take her for her shower," the nurse said.

"I need to head out," Jon said and lowered to kiss Ellen on the cheek.

He heard Charlie say goodbye and kiss her, and together they walked out of the room and down the hall.

"Thank you," Jon said. "I didn't know what to tell her."

"It's okay. Tomorrow she might know, or she might not."

"I didn't expect her to know me."

Charlie laughed. "She didn't know me when I walked in. Maybe you were just far enough back in her memory that it sparked."

"I should come by more."

"Only if you're comfortable," Charlie said.

"There you are," Leona's voice had both men looking up. "I'm ready to get out of here," she said, and then it was as if she noticed Charlie. "Oh, hi, Charlie."

"Hello," Charlie said with a smile. "Well, I'd better get back to it. I have a final paper coming up. I'll see you both later."

He gave a wave and kept walking.

"Was he visiting his grandmother?" Leona asked.

Jon nodded. "Ready to go?"

LEONA WALKED NEXT TO JON, HER ARMS CROSSED IN FRONT OF HER, his head low. Weren't they a pair, she thought.

"Here," she said, handing him the piece of paper her father had given her.

"What is this?" Jon asked as he looked down at it.

"That's what he'll take for the building."

Jon stopped walking. "Why would he sell it to me? If he owns it, you would be next in line to get it, right? I mean, first, this isn't even the going rate for this building, and trust me, I know."

Leona wiped at her eyes because tears had sprung up and rolled down her cheeks. "He'd rather donate the building, or let it crumble around him than to let me take care of it or inherit it. So, you should take him up on it," she said, now walking faster.

Jon reached for her and stopped her in the parking lot. "Whoa," he said, turning her toward him. "Leona, did you look at this paper?"

She nodded.

"This is half of what it's worth. You should have that building."

"He won't give it to me or sell it to me." She wiped her cheeks. "It's okay. This is how he feels."

Jon pulled her into him, wrapping his arms around her. Instinct said she should pull back, but with her cheek pressed against his firm chest, his arms holding her to him, she couldn't.

"That's not fair," Jon said.

"Fair or not, it's how he feels. He blames me for, well, for everything."

His cheek rested on top of her head, and Leona closed her eyes and breathed in the scent of him—the comfort.

"Whatever it is, he's wrong," Jon said. "I'm sure there isn't anything inside you that could possibly cause anyone harm enough to be that angry."

Leona eased back and looked up into Jon's dark eyes. At that moment, her heart ached differently. No one had ever settled her as Jon had with his soft words, and his arms wrapped around her.

Was there such a thing as love at first sight—or third? Leona had made a living off of happily ever afters, but she wasn't sure she'd ever get hers. Until that very moment, no one had ever made her feel as Jon Ford had.

CHAPTER 50

WHEN CHARLIE HAD CALLED OUT HIS GOODBYE TO THE TWO OF them, Leona had quickly moved away from Jon, and then hurried to her car.

"You did agree to dinner on Saturday, right?" Jon asked as he folded himself into her car.

"Yes."

"I'm driving," he said, and now, she couldn't help but laugh.

The air seemed lighter somehow as they drove back to the bookstore.

"So, you know Charlie?" Leona asked, and she noticed him shift uncomfortably in his seat.

"Yeah."

One thing Leona had learned fairly quickly, Jon Ford was not a man of many words. "He's a good kid."

That caused him to turn his head. "He's a grown man."

"Maybe it's the hair. He seems young to me."

Jon nodded. "His grandfather had hair just like that."

At the stop light, she turned to him. "You knew Charlie McGowan?"

His face contorted, but his eyes looked forward and never at her. "Yeah."

"They met in my store. Sadie and Charlie's, that is," she confirmed.

"Is that so?"

Leona nodded as the light turned green, and finally the lightness in her heart was back. That lightness she'd had to train herself to feel.

"The people who come into my bookstore get their happily ever afters," she said proudly.

"That must have been what happened, then," his voice was low enough she wasn't sure she'd heard him.

"What happened?"

He shook his head. "Nothing."

The rest of the ride back was silent until Leona's phone rang three blocks from the store.

She managed it from her purse, which sat on the console between the seats.

"Hello?" she said, knowing the call was from the store by the ringtone.

"Leona!" Sadie shouted. "Water! There's water! Everywhere!"

"What's going on?" she shouted back as she turned the next corner a bit too aggressively.

"Pipe broke," Sadie said, and it was obvious she was moving about.

"I'll be there in two minutes," she said, disconnecting the call and pushing down on the gas pedal. "The pipe in the store broke," Leona managed, and Jon let out a curse.

"I told him. I told that…" he stopped short of aiming that curse right at her father, Leona knew.

Leona skidded into the parking space behind the store. How he managed, she'd never know, but Jon was out of the small car and through the back door before she'd turned off the engine.

As she climbed out of the car, her skirt caught on the emergency brake, and then her purse strap was caught in the door as she slammed it. It took her another moment to get the fob to work to unlock the now locked door and pull her purse out as she stumbled toward the back door.

Sadie and Fiona were cursing and crying as they carried stacks of books from one side of the store to the other. Water burst through the pipes like a sprinkler.

Jon was nowhere.

"The romance section! The romance section!" Sadie shouted as she pointed to a new leak that had sprung above them.

Leona ran toward the shelf of Fiona's books and began to gather as many as she could. The shuffling of books from one shelf to the front door felt as if it had taken an hour, but when the water stopped and Jon reappeared, she knew it had only been a few minutes.

Looking around, Leona's lip began to tremble.

So much that she'd worked so hard for was lost.

Her breath caught in her lungs, white light flickered in front of her, and her knees suddenly gave out.

JON MOVED TOWARD HER, GRIPPING HER ARMS AND HOLDING HER up. "Hey, now," he said and Leona's eyes fluttered up at him.

Fiona took the stack of books from her hands and Jon pulled her to him.

"Come back to me, doll," his voice was warm against her cheek.

"Don't...call me...that," Leona panted against him, and he smiled.

"Yeah, you're okay."

He knew the other two women had stopped their rescue process and were watching them.

"Can you stand?" he asked, and Leona pushed back, but he felt her body go liquid in his arms.

Wrapping an arm tightly around her back, he scooped her legs out from under her and carried her out of the store and to his pickup out front.

He managed the door, and slid her inside. "Sit here for just a moment," he said as he brushed a curl from her face as she sobbed.

"It's all gone."

"Not all of it. Don't move."

Jon walked back to the store and the two women still stood there looking at him. "I'm going to take her home, get her fed, and get her calm. I'll put a call into the catastrophe company, and they'll be out here today. The apartments are flooded too, but I have guys enroute to help out already. The water is off, so we won't have more flooding."

Both women nodded.

The younger one, Charlie's fiancée, he remembered, stepped toward him. "I've never seen her like this."

Jon looked out the window, and he could see Leona's entire body moving as she sobbed. "I've seen this kind of thing before. It's shock. This is her entire life."

"I didn't know you knew each other," Charlie's fiancée said, and Jon wished he could remember her name.

"I don't. I didn't." He let out a breath as he looked out the window. No, he didn't know her, but in his heart he felt a connection to her that he'd only ever felt with one other person. Was it possible that in less than twenty-four hours he could know what that feeling was? He didn't believe in happily ever afters, as the sign on the door said. He hadn't gotten one, so why would he believe in it?

But there was something about Leona that made him want one.

Jon looked around the store. Leona had been right, it was all gone. The smell of wet paper and wood sunk into him.

He tunneled his fingers through his hair. No, he promised himself, it would be better. He was going to buy the building, and they'd rebuild it the way they wanted it, him and Leona. Maybe the *Happily Ever After Bookstore* was his happily ever after.

CHAPTER 51

"Where are we going?" Leona asked, as Jon climbed into the truck and started the engine.

"To your house. Tell me how to get there."

Leona wiped her cheeks. "Why? I need to get in there and clean my store. I have so much to do," she wept again.

Jon reached across the cab of the truck and took her hand in his. "We're going to go to your house and call insurance and catastrophe. We have a lot of work ahead of us. But you need to gather your composure and get changed."

She looked down at her wet skirt and realized he was right.

Then, she looked at their clasped hands and warmth zipped up her arm.

Jon pulled away from the curb, maneuvering the large truck with one hand.

"Why are you taking care of me like this? You don't owe my father anything to take care of that building or my store."

His thumb brushed over her knuckles. "I know."

"You know? What does that mean? I'm not sure you even like me, so why would you want to take time to help me?"

He eased the truck to a stop at the stop sign at the end of the street, pulled his hand from hers, and put the truck in park.

Yep, she thought. She was right. He didn't like her. He was going to make her get out of his truck and he was drive off and leave her in the street. Wasn't this what always happened? When she would get happily ever afters for someone else, she could celebrate. But when everything in her own life turned upside down, she argued and cried, and...

Jon turned in his seat, cupped Leona's face between his large, calloused fingers, and pulled her to him. His lips pressed to hers, and she made a noise—what kind, she wasn't sure.

He smiled against her lips, but he didn't pull back. Jon's eyes opened and met hers, which were staring at him.

He was still smiling as he eased back. "I like you just fine. Now tell me how to get to your house."

JON SAT THERE, AT THE STOP SIGN, UNTIL LEONA COULD MANAGE to tell him, "Go right."

He turned and she sat back in her seat.

Okay, the kiss had been uncharacteristic of him. He was much too careful to meet a woman and kiss her the next day. Heck, he was too careful a man to meet a woman and ask her if she wanted to have dinner the same day, but he had.

It felt good to let go just a bit.

Sean and Penny were his whole world, and that wasn't going to stop. But Jon needed something for himself too, and his work just wasn't filling that void anymore.

He winced when he got to the next stop sign. It was going to be another long day, and it would most certainly go into the night. Guilt squeezed in his chest. He'd need to call his parents for help again. As he eased through the intersection, Jon decided he'd make sure to pick up his kids after daycare tomorrow and take them for ice cream. Surely, being with their grandparents for one more night would be joyous. Hadn't Penny sat on his lap that morning while he was trying to get ready, telling him all about the things his mother and father did to spoil them?

He chuckled as he drove.

"Left, left," Leona said and Jon realized he hadn't been listening.

"Sorry."

"It's okay. My head is a little fuzzy. I'm surprised I know where I live."

He chuckled at that. "It'll all be okay. I know the catastrophe company, and they'll take good care of you. They work with most insurance companies. We'll get them going to the building and up to the apartments. I got the water off before it hit the antique store."

"Good."

"When they get to the building, I'll go talk to your dad and let him know…"

"No."

Jon flashed a look in her direction. "He has to know. It's his building."

"Don't tell him."

"Okay."

She pressed her fingers to her eyes. "I'll call his insurance company. I can get them involved."

Jon gave her a moment before he asked more questions. "What's wrong with him? He doesn't look old enough to be in long-term care."

She wiped her nose on the back of her hand, and he thought it awfully endearing.

"Everything."

"Seriously," Jon said, and she turned her sad eyes toward him.

"Make a right, and it's the second house on the left," she instructed, but kept her eyes on him. "I mean it when I say everything."

229

Jon followed her directions and pulled up in front of a small house that was probably as old as the building her store was in. She had to pay a fortune in heat, he thought, as the windows looked as if they were still original decorative glass, as old as the house.

"This is beautiful," he said, and she looked up at the house.

"It's been in the family for generations."

"How many?"

Leona tucked a curl behind her ear and her bracelets jingled together. "Four."

"That's incredible."

She nodded as she opened the door and stepped out.

Jon climbed from the other side and skirted the front of the truck as Leona walked up the front steps, pulling her key out of her purse.

"I live mostly on the second floor," she said as she slid the key in the lock. "We'll go straight up there."

"Okay," Jon eased out the word.

"Just, well…" Leona let out a breath as she pushed open the door, and he could smell the age of the house and the four generations that had passed through. "Just head upstairs."

Jon stepped into the house and was met with a wall of newspapers stacked by the door, as well as boxes of old books. The musty smell of old things and dust surrounded him.

Desperately wanting to look around, he did as she'd instructed and walked directly up the stairs to the next landing, which already had a light and airy feel to it, a stark contrast to the first floor.

He hadn't seen much of the downstairs, but he knew it had dark wood and decorative wallpaper. Upstairs was white. White walls, repaired wood, area rugs, and new furniture.

"We can sit in the sunroom," Leona said and directed him back toward the front of the house.

The room was flooded with April sun. A small open window allowed for fresh air to filter through.

There was a sofa and a wing-back chair near a coffee table. A small TV sat on a table in the corner.

She had a dining room table to the side of the room, and a small kitchenette. The room was eclectic, just as she was, but it was all her, he could feel it, and it was a stark contrast to what he'd seen of the rest of the house.

"We can work at the table. Would you like coffee or water?"

"I'll take some water," he said as he pulled out a chair and sat down.

"My father never allowed me to move anything out of the house. That's why the downstairs…"

"Leona," he said her name softly, and she looked up at him. "You don't have to explain it or be embarrassed by it."

She nodded, and he knew he'd stopped her from doing just that.

CHAPTER 52

WITHIN THE HOUR, THEY HAD MADE ALL THE PHONE CALLS THEY needed to make. Claims were initiated, and catastrophe crews were headed to the building. Affected tenants had been called, and Jon had secured them places to stay for the night as well.

Leona had called her father, but she hadn't explained the full extent of the problems to him, and Jon wondered why. Perhaps he wouldn't have argued with the man either had he known his condition—then again, what was his condition?

And if Leona had enough control over the building, why couldn't she have approved the repairs that needed to be done?

"I'm going to go change," Leona said after she'd disconnected her last call.

Jon nodded, looking down at the notes he'd taken on the legal pad she'd given him.

A few minutes later, Leona returned from the room down the hall in what Jon would assume was yoga attire. At least that's what his wife would call it when she dressed like that.

Under those long flowy skirts, Leona had been hiding a pair of slim legs, and under those cotton blouses, a set of sculpted, toned arms. She'd taken off her bracelets and rings and pulled back that mass of curls into a ponytail. Something knotted in Jon's stomach when he saw the lotus tattoo at the base of her neck.

It surprised him as much as seeing her in bright orange sneakers.

Pulling on an oversized sweatshirt, she looked up at him when her head came through the top hole, which was cut wide showing off her neck and a shoulder. "What?" she asked.

"You look like a completely different person," he said.

"Well, this is me too."

"It's nice," he said and there was a flash of what he considered irritation that crossed her face. "The catastrophe team already has one of their managers at your store with Fiona and Sadie."

"Already?"

"This is what they do. We'll need to box up everything, so you can assess what needs to be replaced."

He saw the color drain from her face. "I'm out of business, aren't I?"

"Just for a little while. I don't think you're the kind of woman who lets setbacks stop them from doing anything."

Tears were pooling in her eyes and Jon moved to her, pulling her against him again.

"Seriously, it'll only be for a bit. I'll get to work on the building as soon as I can," he promised, enjoying the feel of her against him.

"Why would you even—"

"Let me worry about that."

❧

LEONA WALKED IN THROUGH THE BACK DOOR OF THE STORE, AFTER Jon had parked his truck next to her car behind the building. The smell of the store hit her first. Waterlogged books, damp wood, soaked drywall. Tears hit her second. Anger took over from there.

Jon had warned her father that such a thing would happen, and her father ignored the warning. Well, wasn't he the king of ignoring things? His wife. His child. His health. His business.

The tears dried on her cheeks.

Leona had done everything she could for that man, even trying to understand that earlier that day, he'd offered to nearly give Jon Ford the stupid building she'd been asking to buy for a decade. What good would it do for Jon to buy it now?

"They're moving the fans in through—" his voice stopped behind her. "Leona?"

She realized she'd never even stepped into the store. She was still in the back room, her fists held to her side so tight that her knuckles were white, and her jaw hurt from clenching it.

Spinning to face him, she knew her face must have resonated what was burning through her, because Jon took a step back.

"What's wrong?" he asked.

"You warned him this was going to happen. You told him it needed to be fixed," Leona spat out the words.

"It will get fixed."

"It's already ruined!" she shouted. "Lives have been ruined, when there was no reason for it."

Now Jon stepped to her, reaching for her hands and unfisting them into his. "You need to breathe. Your face is bright red and there is a vein on the side of your head that I'm afraid might burst."

She looked up into his eyes. "I'm so angry."

He nodded slowly. "You should be. But, there's a lot of work to do. You're right, lives have been interrupted, but they're not ruined. Let's get them back on track."

Leona drew in a few deep breaths. "Why do you want to help us?"

Jon reached a hand to her face and brushed his thumb over

her cheek. "I don't know. You've gotten under my skin somehow."

"I met you yesterday," she whispered.

"You did. And yet you're letting me touch you like this."

Leona took a breath to speak, but what was she going to say? She was completely taken by this man that she didn't even know.

"Insurance is going to take a while to come through. I can't rebuild my inventory. I'll be shut down for a long time," her voice was but a whisper.

Jon stepped even closer, his other hand coming to her waist. Leona lifted her hands to his chest.

"It won't be as long as you think." His thumb was still on her cheek. "Trust me, Leona. Will you trust me?"

Gazing up into his dark eyes, she couldn't think of a reason not to—except that she didn't know him at all.

"I'll trust you," the words came from her, and he smiled.

"Good. I'm going to get things settled here, and then I'll be back in a few hours. We'll get a roll-off ordered so you can throw out what's been ruined, but take inventory of it. You'll need that for insurance."

The tears stung her eyes again when she thought about throwing away books.

"You'll be back?" she asked, and her voice quivered.

"I promise."

CHAPTER 53

Jon helped Leona and the others get settled on what they needed to do. The catastrophe team had shown up and worked with the apartment tenants and Leona to get fans started, and the demo figured out.

His wife wasn't a crier, and he found it odd that he seemed to be able to calm Leona when she'd cry because he didn't have experience with that.

By the time he'd left, Leona seemed to have a different attitude about getting to work on the mess they'd been left.

Jon pulled into the parking lot of the bank, the torn piece of paper in his pocket that Leona had handed him.

The price her father had written on the paper was half of what the building was worth. There was no reason to offer Jon the building for that price, except to not let Leona have it.

It had taken him a few phone calls to get the money into the right accounts, but he'd managed it out of earshot of Leona. Now, he'd have a check drawn to buy the building, and he'd head to see Leona's father.

An hour later, Jon was standing in the commons area with Leona's father looking over the check. An hour after that, Jon was headed back to the bookstore. A signed letter saying that the building was his.

LEONA, FIONA, AND SADIE HAD STACKED BOOKS INTO PILES IN THE driest part of the store. There were ruined copies of new books and ruined copies of used books. Likewise, there was a pile of saved books that had no damage, both used and new.

Fiona thumbed through a soaked version of Charlie and Ellen McGowan's book. "Why does this hurt so much? It's paper. They still print this book. It's replaceable. Heck, it's digital. The words are still in the order I put them in, the story still remains."

Sadie lifted a ruined copy of *Gone With the Wind*. "You're right. But it feels as if something sacred was stolen."

Leona wiped the back of her hand across her cheek. "Looking at all of this, and hearing you say that it's just paper makes me think that so much of this was just being held on to."

Both women shifted a confused glance at her.

"What does that mean?" Fiona asked.

Leona adjusted on the Home Depot bucket she'd turned upside down and was using for a stool. "I mean, this was a bookstore when I took it over. It was all used books and knick-knacks. An extension of the antique store. But it wasn't mine from the start. I didn't create it."

Sadie raised an eyebrow. "Sure you did."

Leona laughed now as she looked at the damage surrounding them. "No. I mean I've been so trained not to touch anything in my life, I didn't. Oh, you should see my house." She laughed more. "Something like this should happen there."

Fiona and Sadie exchanged looks before Fiona rested a hand on Leona's leg. "Are you okay?"

"Finally, I am." She wiped away tears on the sleeve of her

sweatshirt as she laughed through them. "See, when my mom died, my father kept everything. I mean everything. My mother's clothes are still in the closet. Any mail that has come to her in the past thirty years is in a box. If she read a book, he kept it."

Leona stood and dropped a few more books into the ruined pile.

"But it didn't stop with her and her memory. My grand-mother did the same thing, and her mother. You can't walk through the first floor of my house because it's a museum to people who aren't here anymore. And, yes, you want to remember them, but at what cost?"

She looked at the stack of books that were used and in okay condition, and moved them to the trash pile.

"We need to remember those who have gone before us, but preserving their lives as if they are here keeps us from living. I never moved a shelf in this store because when the man who owned it died, I didn't know how to touch his things. Everything is just as he'd left it."

Fiona stood and moved to Leona. "Maybe you should get some rest."

"No. I have to clean it out and make it mine. I need to choose colors. I need to bring in books I like. I need to find the shelves I want." She laughed. "I hate that front door."

Now Sadie laughed and Fiona did the same.

"Well, then," Fiona pulled Leona in for a hug. "We'd better get busy."

~

JON PULLED UP IN FRONT OF HIS PARENTS' HOUSE AND HIS MOTHER met him at the door.

"I thought you needed us to pick them up and keep them today," she said.

"I'll need you to keep them. I have something I want to talk about first, and then I'll go pick them up and bring them over."

His mother reached her hand out and touched his arm. "Jon, is everything okay?"

He smiled. "Everything is wonderful."

At the kitchen table, Jon told his parents about buying the building. His mother was more than familiar with the bookstore and the antique store.

"Stacy used to love the bookstore," she said with her hand pressed to her chest. "We'd go to author readings and events there."

Jon nodded. "She did love it." He took a moment to suck in that memory. "Leona, who owns the store, says that everyone who visits her store gets their happily ever after."

"Isn't that sweet," his mother said.

"I figure that's why Stacy and I were so happy. She read books from the store."

"That's a nice thought."

"I think the store is my happily ever after too," he said, and his parents exchanged looks.

"Because you'll own the building?" his father asked.

"Actually, I think I'm in love with Leona, the owner."

CHAPTER 54

Jon waited for his parents to react. They sat silent for a few moments. His mother fidgeted with the tablecloth, and his father eased back into his chair and crossed his arms in front of him.

"You're in love with someone?" his mother finally managed.

"I think I am," Jon said, smiling. "No, I know I am."

His father's brows drew together. "I haven't heard you talk about anyone. Where have you been keeping her?"

Jon watched his mother twist the cloth in her hands, and he reached his hand out to cover hers and calm her.

"I just found her. I met her yesterday."

His mother moved her hands from his and stood to fidget in the kitchen with items on the counters.

"I know this sounds weird," Jon said. "But I've been in love before, so I know how it feels. I get the same feeling resonating inside of me, just as it did when Stacy was around."

His mother began to fill the sink with water and soap. "It's not just you now, Jon."

"I know that," he said as he stood and walked to his mother.

"And the kids are a dealbreaker. I mean if they don't like her, or she's not the motherly type..."

His mother turned. "Are you trying to replace Stacy?"

Jon reached across his mother and turned off the faucet. "Mom," he said, taking her shoulders and turning her toward him. "No one will ever replace Stacy. I loved Stacy with every ounce of my being. Look what she gave me," he said, feeling the emotion of it tighten his chest. "But she's gone, and I'm still here. I haven't even considered finding another woman or dating. But then yesterday, I met Leona, and..."

His mother shook her head and wiped a tear that rolled over her cheek. "This sounds like that story you once told me about Stacy's grandparents."

Jon laughed. "Ellen and Charlie?"

"Yes."

"True and spontaneous love," he said softly.

"What if that kind of love isn't real?"

"What if it is?" He pulled his mother to him and held her. "I saw her today. Ellen."

"Isn't she in a memory care facility?"

Jon nodded, pressing a kiss to the top of his mother's head and taking a step back. "She is. And, I don't know how, but she remembered me."

"Are you sure?"

"She called me by name, asked about the kids, and told me to have Stacy stop by and see her."

His mother pressed a hand to her chest. "Oh, dear. What did you tell her?"

"Charlie, her grandson, told her that Stacy worked late hours. She seemed okay with that, and he thought it was the best answer."

Jon's father stood and walked toward them. "It sounds like you have a lot of wonderful things going on in your life," he said, coming to stand behind Jon's mother, resting his hands on her shoulders.

"I do. Of course, I'm going to need some extra help for a while. Leona's store was flooded, as were some of the units of the building. We're going to have to rebuild."

His father chewed his lip. "Are you going to need some help rebuilding?"

Jon smiled. "I just might."

JON TOOK HIS MOTHER'S MINIVAN TO PICK UP HIS KIDS.

"Why did you bring Nana's car?" Penny asked, as Jon walked hand in hand with his children across the parking lot.

"She had your seats. I have to go back to work."

"Nana and Papa's house?" Sean asked.

"Yes, we're going to their house. You're going to stay there again tonight."

Penny looked up at him. "Are you going to sleep on the couch again?"

Jon laughed. "I don't know."

"I don't think you should. It should just be our thing we get to do," Penny told him.

Jon stopped at the minivan and pulled open the sliding door. Sean jumped inside, but Penny studied him.

"You really don't want me there?"

Penny kicked a small rock at her feet. "If you want to, I guess it's okay. But, we love to spend the night there. It's special."

Jon waited until Penny jumped up into the van, and he kissed her head. "It is special. I'm glad you enjoy being there."

"What are you going to be doing?" Sean asked, as Jon began to buckle him into his seat.

"I have a friend whose business had a lot of water flood her store. I'm going to be helping her put her store back together."

"What kind of store?" Penny asked as she put her arms through her harness.

"A bookstore."

Penny's eyes went wide. "I love books."

And that was because she was just like her mother.

"I know you do."

"Will you bring me a book?"

Jon laughed. "Most of them were ruined. But I'll ask her if there are any that are okay."

"I'm getting a book!" Penny cheered.

"I want a book, too," Sean cheered.

Jon kissed his head and then checked Penny's seat.

He closed the door and walked around to the driver's door. As he opened it, he realized he hadn't mentioned that he had children to Leona yet. Perhaps he should do that soon.

His feelings had taken over, and he'd thought about the well-being of his kids, but he hadn't thought about the surprise it might be to Leona. What would she think of his little family?

She'd already misjudged the situation with their babysitter, though Jon hadn't helped her understand it.

CHAPTER 55

JON PULLED UP AND PARKED IN THE FRONT OF THE BOOKSTORE. HE sat in his truck for a moment, looking into the store.

It pained him to think the store was in disarray. Shelves were pulled away from the walls and inventory was in boxes to be disposed of.

Jon was used to fixing things. But he'd never built anything and then watched it be destroyed.

There was a tightness in his chest and he realized that was wrong. He'd built a relationship with a woman, married her, built a family with her, and then watched as his world crumbled into a darkness he couldn't rebuild.

Thanks to his parents, he'd at least come out of the isolation he'd put himself into. And now, he was enamored with a woman that made him feel fresh and new, just like her store would be.

He stepped out of his truck and walked to the front door, only to have it open before he reached it.

The fans from inside whirred, and it made his head pound.

Leona stepped outside and closed the door behind her. "It's horribly noisy in there," she said with a laugh and Jon thought that strange, especially since he'd left her in tears.

"It'll be that way for the next week."

"I'll bring headphones," she joked again.

"I'm so sorry this happened," Jon said, and he felt it in his core. As if he could have prevented this if her father had only listened.

Leona shrugged. "What's done is done. When she's all put back together, she's going to shine like a new penny."

Jon studied her. No, this wasn't the same woman he'd left there earlier, he thought.

"Where is everyone?"

Leona turned and looked at the store. "I sent them home. Really, what are we going to accomplish? When the dumpster gets here, we'll start throwing out the ruined and planning for the new."

That resonated with him.

She resonated with him.

Jon moved to her, and she didn't shift or move away.

Placing his hand on her waist, he pulled her to him, and easily, as if they'd done it a thousand times, Leona lifted her arms around his neck.

This time, it wasn't him who moved in, it was her.

She cupped her hands at the nape of his neck and drew him down to her. Her lips brushed over his, and when he parted them, she held on a little tighter and dove into the kiss she was offering.

Jon staggered them back to the closed door and pressed her against it. The afternoon sun beat down on his back, and he was fully aware of the traffic on the street around them, but he just didn't care.

Leona's tongue ran over his bottom lip and then moved against his.

Now both of his hands were on her waist, like an anchor, so he could push back at any moment. But he didn't push back.

"Sorry," she said now as she eased back from the kiss, but stayed close, her forehead pressed against his.

"For what?"

"Kissing you like that."

"No need to be sorry," he said, still a little out of breath. "I didn't expect to come back, and have you be in this good of a mood."

"I had some clarity about my life," she admitted as she drew back and looked up at him.

"I can't wait to hear about it."

She eased from him and took his hand. Their fingers linked together as if they'd held hands like that their entire lives.

"Come in. I'll tell you all about it."

Leona kept her hand tucked into Jon's and opened the door to the store. He followed her, and she proceeded to tell him about the epiphany she'd had about starting from scratch—something that was truly hers.

She was shouting over the fans. Her arms waved in dramatic fashion as she told him of color schemes, shelving, book sections, lighting, and whatever else crossed her mind.

When she was done, she turned to him, only to find him standing in the middle of the wet room grinning at her.

"What do you think?" she asked.

"I think you're beautiful."

She felt her mouth open and her eyes widen. She hadn't expected that.

"Thank you."

He took a step toward her, lifting her hand to his lips. "I think this all sounds wonderful," he said, and then pulled her into his arms. One hand on her waist, the other still holding her hand, he swayed them in a dance to music no one could hear. "I want to be part of it."

"You do?"

"I do," he said, lowering his mouth to hers.

"What are we doing?" She stopped swaying, but he didn't let go. "We met yesterday morning."

"You know the story of Ellen and Charlie McGowan, right?"

"And you knew Charlie McGowan," she reminded him, narrowing her eyes on him.

"I did. And he was one of the finest men I'd ever met."

"So, you don't think this is too fast, if you're of his state of mind."

Jon laughed. "Right," he said, swaying against her again and she followed. "I want to be your partner in all of this."

Leona stopped now and took that step back to separate them. "Why?"

"Because I want to do something with this building. Because I love hearing you talk about what can be in this space. Because I feel something for you that I thought was lost in me forever."

Her lips began to tremble. "Jon..."

He moved to her, taking her hands into his. "I mean it. I didn't think I could love again, but..."

"Don't."

"Leona..."

"Don't say something like that." She pressed her hand to her chest. "I'm beginning to think Charlie McGowan was crazy."

She laughed after she said it, and so did he.

Jon moved to her again. "I won't say it like that. But here," he said, and he pulled a piece of paper from his pocket. "I want us to make this legally a fifty-fifty deal."

"What are you talking about?"

Jon handed her the paper and Leona unfolded it. "This is a bill of sale."

"I gave your dad a check today."

She lifted her eyes to him. "This isn't legally binding. He can't sign legal papers while he's in the facility."

Jon nodded. "I thought about that too. He still has the check, but I figured you were his power of attorney?"

Leona worried her bottom lip. "No."

Jon's eyes widened. "Well then, I might have given my money to the wrong person."

"I think we'll be okay. I'll talk to him, my father's power of attorney." She folded the paper. "You really did this?"

"I did."

"Why?"

"For all those reasons I gave you. I want to be your partner."

Leona studied him. His dark eyes did something to her, she couldn't explain. This man, this gruff and cranky man who wore work boots and drove a pickup truck, twisted her insides enough she could believe Charlie McGowan's thoughts on instant love.

"You don't just mean in this building, do you?" her question was breathy.

Jon wrapped her in his arms again, pressing a kiss to her lips. "No. I don't."

"Wow," she let the word out on a breath.

"Yeah, wow."

CHAPTER 56

WHILE JON WALKED THROUGH THE RESIDENTIAL UNITS, AND MET with the antique store owner, Leona sat in her car, where it was quiet, and called her uncle.

"Leona, my sweet niece. It's so good to hear from you," her uncle's voice rang out over the phone.

"Hi, Uncle George," she said softly.

George was her father's older brother, but in stark contrast to her father, he was healthy and strong of mind—and he doted on Leona.

"What's new, sweet-pea?"

"I need to talk to you about the building my dad owns."

She heard George sigh. "Why does he hold onto that dang thing? Do you know I get calls all the time, people wanting to buy it."

"I'm sure," she agreed. "Well, it appears he did sell it."

Her uncle let out a hum. "He can't do that."

"I know, and that's why I'm calling you." She tapped her fingers on her steering wheel. "You know he won't sell it to me. Or even give it to me."

"Stubborn old man," her uncle said, and she chuckled at that.

"Well, he offered to sell it to Jon Ford."

"No kidding?" her uncle's words were drawn out.

"You know Jon Ford?"

"I know of him," he said. "How much did he say he'd take for it?"

"Less than half of what it's worth."

"And Ford jumped on that?" his voice hinted at irritation.

Leona pulled down her visor and lifted the mirror on the back. Looking at herself, she wondered how much she was going to tell her uncle. Then she thought again, she'd tell him everything. Though, even she didn't believe what the past two days had brought to her.

"Jon took Dad a check and had a bill of sale."

"Not legal," he amended.

"We've discussed that."

"You and Jon Ford?"

"Yes."

"How do you know him?"

Leona closed up the visor. "He was fixing a plumbing leak in one of the apartments."

"I told your father to get that fixed."

"Well, he didn't. The pipe burst and ruined my store and the apartment above me."

She heard her uncle groan. "Oh, Leona. I'm so sorry. I should have—"

"You couldn't have done anything. I know that."

"It's completely ruined?"

"Completely," she said. "But it'll be a good new start. I mean, it'll be all mine, not what was already there."

"But Jon wants to buy it and your father agreed?"

"He did."

"And what about you? Leona, it should be your building. You deserve it."

"I agree, but," she bit down on her cheek. "Well," she stammered. "Jon wants to buy it, but he wants to go in fifty-fifty with me on ownership. He wants to be my business partner."

Her uncle was quiet at the other end of the line for a moment.

"Jon Ford wants to be your business partner?"

"Yes."

"How well do you know him?"

She felt the tension in her belly knot again. "I'm kind of seeing him."

"Kind of?"

"It's new."

"Well, now. That's interesting."

Leona wiped her hand down the leg of her yoga pants.

"What do you think?" she asked her uncle.

"Is it what you want, honey? If this thing with you and Jon Ford doesn't work..."

"I know. It's a risk."

Her uncle clucked his tongue. "I'll get it in motion, honey. Bring Jon around, and we'll get things started."

That knot in Leona's stomach loosened. "Thank you."

"I think you deserve to be happy. I love you, kiddo."

"I love you too."

JON WALKED THROUGH THE FRONT OF THE STORE AS LEONA WALKED through the back. They met in the middle, the soggy floor giving under their feet.

"How did it go?" he asked.

"My uncle said he'd make it happen," she offered, and Jon's arms wrapped around her, pulling her in.

"Will you be my partner?" he asked, lowering his lips to her jaw.

"I think we need to discuss it more."

"Of course," he said as he trailed kisses from her ear down her neck, and over her collarbone. "We'll discuss it."

"Jon," Leona said, bracing her hands on his chest.

He lifted his head and looked down at her. "What's wrong?"

"My head is spinning."

"Maybe it's the fans."

She shook her head. "No, it's you. It's all you."

His gaze narrowed on her. "Too fast?"

Leona sucked her lips between her teeth. "I really feel as if I'm too old to say yes."

Jon laughed. "I'll slow down."

"No, I don't think I want to do that either."

They broke apart when the front door chimes rang over the sound of the fans. Amber walked into the store and her eyes went wide, though Leona was quite sure it was the state of the store, and not that she'd seen them.

"Oh, wow!" she said, looking around. "What happened here?"

"Burst pipe," Jon said as he tucked his hands into his front pockets.

"I'm so sorry," Amber directed the comment to Leona. "If I can be of help getting it back in order, let me know. My mom will be devastated."

"Thank you. We'll be rebuilt in no time," Leona said.

Amber nodded and then turned her attention back to Jon. "Mr. Ford, I saw your truck and thought I'd come find you. I won't be able to come over this Saturday."

"It's okay," he said quickly, shifting a glance between Amber and Leona. "We'll be good."

Amber nodded then looked at Leona. "Really, though, anything we can do to help…"

"I'll let you know."

Amber turned and walked out of the store at the same time Jon's phone rang. He pulled it from his pocket and walked out the back door.

Leona stood in the middle of the room, the fans whirring around her.

What was it about Amber's presence that made Jon seem secretive, she wondered? It was further proof that no one knew someone well enough within twenty-four hours to be kissing them, as they had been, or to go into business with them.

CHAPTER 57

"The dumpster will be here tomorrow," John said as he walked back into the store, tucking his phone into his pocket.

"Good," Leona said, wrapping her arms around herself. "I'm ready to start over."

"It'll be at least a month, maybe two to get the pipes redone and the walls and…"

"I know." Tears filled her eyes. Not because she was afraid of the work that would be involved, but because at that moment she was overwhelmed. "I'll be here to do whatever I need to do."

Jon moved toward her, pulling her into his arms. "What's wrong?"

"It's just a lot. And we haven't even had but a moment to take this all in. I mean, everything is lost. I want the repairs done now. I want the store I've always dreamed of. Add to that, you want to buy the building."

"Did buy the building," he amended. "And I want your name on it."

She shook her head. "It's all backward. He should have just let me have the building, but he wouldn't even consider it. But you, a stranger, he'd sell it to you—almost give it to you."

Jon eased back. "Are you mad at me for that?"

"No. I'm mad at him. I'm mad that I didn't see what he was doing to me all this time. The fact that you're the first person I've had in my home—ever," she choked out the words. "I'm embarrassed."

"Don't be."

"How can I not be? It makes me sick. I don't even want to go home now that I see how I was living."

Jon bit down on his bottom lip. "You could go home with me tonight."

The thick, damp air caught in Leona's chest. "Yesterday I didn't know you. I'm not sure that I even liked you."

"Good first impressions are not my strongest asset."

She pressed her hand to her forehead. "But now we're kissing and talking about partnerships and Charlie McGowan…"

"He was wise."

"Stop!" she shouted, though she didn't mean to. "It's too much."

Jon rocked back on his heels, shoving his hands back into his pockets again. "Okay. I get it."

"No. No, I don't think you do." Tears were streaming down her face and she hated the many emotions she was going through. "I'm mad at my father. So mad—you just have no idea."

Leona picked up a stack of books and threw them into a box.

"And I'm mad at myself for never moving a dang thing in this store to make it my own."

She pushed back her hair and continued.

"And I'm mad that I can't let go and just love you—a perfect stranger."

Jon watched her carefully. "Do you want to love me?"

"I don't know. It's the craziest thing I've ever considered in my whole life."

"Because you think Charlie McGowan was crazy?"

"Yes. No." She threw her hands up. "This has nothing to do with Charlie McGowan."

Jon smiled. "No, it doesn't."

"Do you really think you love me?" she asked, though he'd skirted around the words as she'd told him to do.

Jon nodded. "I really do."

"How do you know that?"

Jon raked his fingers through his hair and scratched his head. "Because I've been in love before. I know how it feels to be in the presence of someone and the whole world is right, even when it's crumbling around you."

"Well, I've never been in love. I've hardly dated. I'm just some spinster that…"

"You're certainly not that."

"You saw my house."

"You hate your house."

"I love my house. I hate the past living in it with me."

He nodded. "So, we'll clean it out."

Leona batted her eyes. "What are we doing?"

Jon moved to her and gathered her in his arms, again. He brushed away a curl from her face that had escaped from her ponytail. "We're falling in love. And I don't think either of us expected it or could stop it."

Leona raised her arms around his neck. "I'm scared to death."

"So am I," he admitted.

"Before we can even consider this, I have to know, what's up with you and Amber?"

JON SWALLOWED HARD. HIS MOUTH WENT DRY, AND THE HEART rate which had been revved up by her saying she might be in love with him thudded like a bass drum in his chest.

This was it.

This was the moment she either loved him more or hated him forever.

"Amber," he said her name hard, as if he had to think harder about it. "Well, she helps me out."

Leona's eyes narrowed coldly on him.

But before he could explain, or she could accuse him or ask questions, a car pulled up in front of the store. The late afternoon sun flickered off of the windshield and drew their attention to the street.

Jon let out a breath. "Well, that's timing," he said.

"Who is that?"

"That would be what Amber helps me out with." He lifted her fingers to his lips and kissed them.

CHAPTER 58

Jon kept Leona's hand wrapped in his as they walked to the door and the side door of the minivan opened.

Penny was already out of her seat and helping Sean get out of his before Jon's parents had a chance to get out.

"We're getting ice cream," Sean shouted, still trapped in his seat.

"Grandma said I could get cookies in mine," Penny said as she finally freed her brother and they both jumped out of the minivan and ran to him.

Jon let go of Leona's hand as he scooped Sean up and balanced him on his hip. Placing a hand on Penny's shoulder, he looked at Leona.

Her eyes had gone wide, and her mouth was open in what he assumed was surprise.

He should have told her. It should have been one of the first things they discussed, especially when Amber had mentioned she could help him.

"Penny, Sean, this is my friend Leona. Can you tell her hello?"

Both of his children looked at her.

Sean rested his head on Jon's shoulder, but Penny gave her a small wave.

"Hi."

Jon watched Leona blink hard and then form a smile on her lips, but it was pained. That was evident.

"Hello," Leona said.

"Why were you holding hands?" Penny looked up at Jon and asked.

Again, he exchanged looks with Leona. "We're special friends," he said.

"Do we get a book?"

"I forgot about that," Jon said. "We'll see."

Jon's parents walked toward them and his mother smiled.

"I'm Delores," she said, holding her hand out to Leona. "I'm Jon's mother. This is Frank, his dad."

Leona shook both of their hands. "It's nice to meet you."

"I'm sorry to hear about your store. I've loved coming here over the years. My daughter-in-law and I would come often," his mother said, and then Delores' eyes went wide. Yeah, she'd felt the sting in her own words, Jon thought.

"I'm sorry I couldn't call you by name. But you are familiar," Leona said.

His mother brushed away the comment. "I'll bet you see hundreds of people a week. How can you keep track of them all? I came to Fiona Gable's book signing. It was so sweet of the coffee shop to bring us drinks while we were waiting."

Leona kept that smile as she nodded. "You and your daughter-in-law came together?" she asked, and Jon knew that was the test.

He set Sean down. "So where are you going for ice cream?" he interrupted the conversation before his mother could answer.

"Bloom's on Main," his mother said. "We knew you'd be here, and we wanted to see if you both could come with us."

Jon nodded. "You guys head down there. We'll be right behind you. We need to lock up."

Sean and Penny took their grandparents' hands and the four of them started up the street.

Leona turned back to the store and immediately began to throw books into boxes.

"Hey," Jon's voice came over the noise of the fans.

"That wasn't uncomfortable at all." She threw down another book. "Yep, Charlie McGowan was an idiot!" she shouted.

Jon turned off the two fans closest to him and the noise was half of what it had been. The other fans still whirred in the background.

"Amber is my babysitter."

"Did you forget you had kids? I mean some young thing says she can come to your house, my mind goes in a certain direction, and you knew it, but no, you couldn't tell me you had kids?"

"I just didn't..."

"What? You didn't know about them? They just came into your life?" She picked up another stack of books and threw them into another box. "My father did that too. I wasn't important to him either. I never met anyone. I didn't know anyone he knew. Heck, I'm not even important enough to inherit this stupid, dilapidated building," she shouted.

"It's not like that."

"I find it interesting that in the span of two days we can eat together and kiss each other, consider a business partnership—oh, and tell one another that we might have fallen in love, but you never mentioned your kids."

Jon raked his fingers through his hair. "I should have."

"Oh, yes, you should have."

"It's not their fault."

"I didn't blame them."

"I do love you, Leona," he said, and she shook her head.

"No. I think this whole thing has been so that you can get into this building."

Jon moved to her, but she stepped back. "I would never do that."

"How do I know that?"

"You have to trust me."

Leona pinched the bridge of her nose. "How?"

"Because you know you do. Because we do love each other, no matter how many days we've known each other."

"And you know all about love because, what, you loved their mother? If you loved her so much, Jon, where is she now? How come you're here kissing me and not raising a family with the woman you love?"

"Because she died giving birth to Sean," he said calmly, but his voice dripped with sadness.

Leona dropped herself onto the Home Depot bucket she'd sat on earlier in the day. With her face in her hands, she sobbed.

What was it with the crying and the emotion?

"I'm so sorry," she said.

Jon knelt down in front of her, his knee on the wet ground. "I should have told you."

"You're raising them alone?"

He nodded. "We do okay. My parents help out—a lot. Amber sits with them on the weekends so I can have some guy time." He took her hands in his again. "And, since my wife was Charlie McGowan's granddaughter, she might think you're wrong in your impression of him."

CHAPTER 59

LEONA STARED UP AT HIM. THE LOST LOOK ON HER FACE MADE JON love her more.

"Your wife was Charlie McGowan's granddaughter?"

Jon nodded. "Yes."

"This is a small, small world."

"And it's full of tiny miracles." He lifted his hand to her cheek. "Not only did I find you yesterday, this morning when we went to visit your dad, I stopped in to see Ellen, and she knew me. She called me by name."

"She did?"

"Charlie said that she didn't even remember him when he'd walked in. But when I walked in, and she knew me, then she knew him too."

"That's amazing."

"I'm going to take it as a sign." Jon brushed away her tears. "A sign that we should be grateful for everything—including meeting new people, broken water pipes, and old men who nearly give away buildings to strangers."

"That's a stretch."

"It's something I'm grateful for. And, when your uncle can

make the sale of the building go through, the title will have both of our names on it. I want this, Leona. I want this for both of us."

"We're crazy, right?"

"Completely."

"What if your kids hate me?"

Jon ran his thumb over her lips. "They won't. They have their mother's heart. They find the good in everything."

Leona laughed. "I don't know that I can live up to the image of your wife."

"You can't," he admitted and watched as her eyes flashed something that could be taken as hurt. "I mean, you're you. You have your own amazing qualities."

"Don't you think you should get to know those qualities before you decide that you love me?"

"No. I think that people waste their time dating and figuring things out. I think if you know you love someone, you should commit to that person, and then learn about them every day. There won't be any getting tired of their stories you've already heard. It'll be new all the time."

Now she laughed. "Like I said, that's a stretch."

"Give me a chance, doll?" he asked with a wink.

"I hate that word."

"Give me a better one."

"Sweetheart. Honey. Girlfriend. Wife."

Jon nodded slowly. "I like that collection."

∼

OF COURSE, HIS KIDS LOVED LEONA. SHE COULD TALK ABOUT books, and stories, and cartoons of all things.

When she'd fallen into conversation with Sean over the glory of chocolate covered raisins, and they'd bonded while eating ice cream, he knew she was the one.

They'd walked back to the store after they'd eaten ice cream, the kids falling in step between them as if it were natural for them to do so.

When Penny mentioned a book, again, and Sean wanted to go into the store, Jon stopped them.

"It's too dangerous to go inside right now," he told them.

Leona rested her hand on his arm. "But let me go in and see what I can find."

A few minutes later, Leona returned with two age-appropriate books that hadn't been ruined. She gave Sean one about dinosaurs, and Penny one about unicorns.

"I love unicorns," Penny beamed.

"I assumed so from your dress."

Penny looked up at her dad. "You're not coming over, right? Grandma and Grandpa can read these for us?"

Jon smiled. "I promise to stay away."

"Good," Penny beamed up at him before she climbed into the minivan where Sean was already buckled into his seat reading his book.

Jon's mother kissed him on the cheek. "So, you're not showing up at my door after I've gone to bed?"

He laughed. "No. I promised Penny not to intrude."

His mother nodded. "Okay." She turned to Leona. "It's been a pleasure getting to know you. I look forward to your store when it reopens. Your plans sound wonderful," she said as she leaned in and kissed Leona on the cheek.

"Thank you."

Jon watched his family drive away with his arm wrapped around Leona's waist.

"They like you," he said.

"I gave them books. What's not to like?"

He pressed a kiss to the top of her head. "I think it was more than that," he said, drawing her into him.

Leona rested her hands on his chest. "Does Penny remember her mother?"

Jon shook his head. "She has pictures and I tell her stories. But, no. She doesn't remember her. She was only a year and a half old when she died."

"I'm so sorry."

Jon brushed his hand over her hair. "It's been a hard three years, but every day they get older and wiser. She's part of them, deep down inside them, and I get to see them grow up. They are the greatest thing that ever happened to me."

"You're a great dad."

"I'm a tired dad. A dad that works too hard, and I'm a little cranky."

Leona laughed. "And that came across the first time I met you."

He couldn't blame her for that. "Let's lock up and go home."

He felt her go rigid in his arms.

"You should go home to your family," Leona said.

"You heard my family. I'm not allowed," he said, smiling down at her.

Leona raised her hand to his stubbled cheek. "If we go home, where do we go?"

"My home is filled with them."

"And my home is filled with everyone else," she said.

Jon lowered his lips to her jaw and skimmed kisses over it. "This has been a very long day," he whispered in her ear. "I think we could use a relaxing atmosphere for our first night together."

Leona let her head fall back to expose her neck, which Jon trailed kisses down. "What did you have in mind?"

"I'll make some calls. Do you like room service?"

CHAPTER 60

THE BOOKSTORE WAS LOUD WITH WHIRRING FANS, NOISY TOOLS, and voices carrying over the other noises.

Aside from the fact that Leona was wearing a pair of old overalls, which she usually painted in, and an old Go Army! T-shirt underneath, sneakers, and her hair pulled back, it was going to be a normal productive day at work.

She carried her cup of coffee, as well as a tray with two others, that Charlie McGowan had made for her, and she strolled into the store at ten o'clock.

The men working on tearing up the old floor never looked her way, but both women whom she adored looked up at her with wide eyes.

Their attire matched hers, in their own way. Yet, dirt streaked on both of their faces since they'd already been hard at work for hours, and she was just arriving.

They weren't mad, Leona deciphered. But they were due a story, and didn't she have one?

Without a word, she nodded to the front door, then walked out of it and toward the bench that sat outside the antique store.

Sadie and Fiona followed and sat down next to her.

"Extra foam for you," Leona handed Fiona a cup.

"Thank you."

"And your fiancé made this special for you," Leona said, handing the cup to Sadie.

"Thank you."

Leona sat back, crossed her legs, pulled on her sunglasses, and sipped her coffee. The other two women watched, and then exchanged glances.

"Okay," Fiona finally said. "Give it up. We haven't seen you since Tuesday. Cryptic texts telling us what workers will be in the store each day is weird. Seriously, have you been in the hospital? Because everything that happened earlier this week would have driven me to being locked up."

Leona laughed into her cup before placing both feet on the ground, and then flashing her left hand at them.

Fiona grabbed her hand. "Leona, that's a diamond."

"Uh-huh."

"That's like a carat and a half."

"Not quite," Leona admitted.

Both women looked up at her with wide eyes, but Sadie was the first to speak. "You got married, didn't you?"

Leona smiled wide, so wide that it nearly hurt. "Yes."

"McGowan syndrome hits again," Fiona said, drawn out.

"Well, he is—was," she corrected, "related to Charlie McGowan."

Fiona looked at Sadie, who nodded. "His late wife was my Charlie's cousin."

"You don't say?" Fiona bobbed her head, still holding on to Leona's hand. "So Leona, the keeper of happily ever afters, got her own?"

"And a son and a daughter."

"He has kids?" Fiona's voice rose as she asked.

Leona pulled her phone from the pocket of the overalls. She scrolled through the photos until she came to one of all four of them.

"Sean is three. Penny is four."

Fiona and Sadie studied the photo taken just the day before in the chamber of the Justice of the Peace. Jon held Sean on his hip, the small boy's arms wrapped tightly around Jon's neck. Leona's hands rested on Penny's shoulders, and the young girl smiled wide, holding her doll, which had belonged to her mother.

Fiona turned to Sadie. "You said his late wife. Their mother died?"

Sadie nodded, but it was Leona that said, "She died during childbirth with Sean."

Fiona's hand pressed into her heart. "That's heartbreaking."

Leona nodded, taking her phone and looking down at her family. "He loved her a lot."

"And does that bother you?"

Leona shook her head. "No. It just tells me he knows how to love completely. And he loves me."

Leona could hardly recognize her own voice. Though she'd always thought she was happy, she realized until that cranky man had walked into her store with bad news, she hadn't known happiness at all.

She'd created it for others. Steering them to books that would bring them joy, or inviting them to a book club where they'd meet someone special, that was her happiness.

Swapping books so that Sadie and Charlie would have to find one another again, or making sure Price was at Fiona's book signing with plenty of time to talk to her, that was her kind of happily ever after skill set.

But running off and getting married while her whole world was turned upside down, now that had been a leap of faith that even a week ago she wouldn't have thought possible.

"I got it! I got it!" Jon's voice boomed from down the street as he hurried toward them waving a piece of paper.

Leona jumped to her feet and ran to her husband, who picked her up and swung her around.

"What did you get?" Fiona asked as she stood from the bench and Sadie followed.

"The building," Leona beamed. "He bought the building."

"And is this a good thing?" Fiona asked.

"The best thing ever," Leona said with a laugh before planting a kiss on her husband's lips. "We're going to make it beautiful again."

EPILOGUE

FIVE MONTHS LATER

THE NOISES BUBBLING FROM THE *HAPPILY EVER AFTER BOOKSTORE* were warm and happy. Music played. People talked. Books were read.

Fiona sat at a table with her newest release, which she'd published under the company she and Price had created. The line to get a signed copy wrapped around the store. Price stood next to her, opening the book to the right page for her to sign. Leona had even seen a few people ask him to sign it too. It was, after all, a story about them—with the names changed, of course.

The display in the corner had a small crowd around it looking at brochures of the new bed and breakfast that Leona and Jon had created in her house, once they'd cleaned out all the old and refurbished the house. Jon's mother would oversee it, for the most part. But her first priority was to Sean and Penny, and Leona agreed that the bed and breakfast came second to those duties.

Amber was going to community college locally, so she had moved into the caretaker's apartment to be there when guests were on site.

Sean was hoisted up on Leona's hip, eating a cookie, which

the owners of the coffee shop had sent down for the grand re-opening celebration.

She kissed his head and took a moment to appreciate his smell. Though both kids had been bathed that morning, Leona had come to learn that little boys exuded a smell of sweat, play, and love, and it mixed into an intoxicating scent.

"Mum," they had come to call her, which was different from Mom, and she was okay with that. "Can I color at the table?"

"Of course," she said, kissing his head one more time before setting him down to run across the store and join his sister in the new children's area.

Jon moved in behind Leona and wrapped his arms around her, resting his chin on her shoulder.

"This is a beautiful store you have here, Mrs. Ford."

"It's everything I ever dreamed of," she said as she looked around at the custom shelves lined with colorful books. The bright area rugs which distinguished each section, and for the fall, leaves hung from a thin fishing line from the ceiling. In the winter, they would put up snowflakes. In spring there would be flowers. And in the summer, maybe beach balls, she wasn't sure yet. All she knew was this was what she'd dreamed of.

The front window had been designed by Sadie, Leona's full-time employee, who had an eye for detail.

Leona looked up to see Sadie and Charlie walking through the store hand in hand and greeting people they knew. They'd been married for two months, and Ellen McGowan had attended the wedding and had known every person there. That night, when Ellen had returned to the memory care facility, she'd gone to sleep and had never awakened. Pressed to her chest was the book Fiona had written about Charlie and Ellen McGowan and their swift and enduring love. Surely Ellen was now with her Charlie, dancing for eternity.

. . .

WHEN THE PARTY HAD ENDED, AND THE STORE WAS CLEANED OF the many people who had celebrated with them, Leona opened a bottle of champagne.

Jon held out a glass for her to fill, and she handed it to Fiona. "Congratulations on your new book, which soared to the top of the charts."

"Thank you," Fiona accepted the glass.

Leona filled another, and handed it to Price. "And to you, sir. Congratulations on your newest song being selected for that hot new movie."

"Thank you," Price took the glass and clinked it to his wife's.

The next glass Leona filled, she handed to Charlie. "Congratulations on your graduation with honors."

"Upcoming graduation."

"It's in the bag," Leona smiled and winked at the man with the mop of white blond hair which gave him a boyish look.

Sadie held up her hand and waved off the glass Leona was going to hand her. "I'll pass."

"We're celebrating. Are you sure?"

Sadie looked up at Charlie, and he wrapped his arm around her shoulders, pulling her in closer.

"I am. Charlie and I have been doing a lot of celebrating today." She took a deep breath. "This morning, I took a pregnancy test, and it came back positive."

There was a collective cheer from everyone in the circle. Fiona rushed to Sadie and pulled her in tight.

"This is the most exciting news," Fiona cheered.

Sadie took Fiona's hands in hers. "Charlie and I've talked about this for a long time," she said, looking into Fiona's eyes. "My dad isn't around. My mom, well, she's not grandmother material. She's hardly mother material."

Charlie kissed Sadie gently on the head and turned his attention to Fiona. "What she's trying to say is, we know your babies all live in heaven. And we pray that this little one will be healthy and happy here on earth with us—"

Fiona wiped a tear from her cheek. "I hope that for you too," she interrupted as Price moved in and wrapped an arm around her.

"—but we'd like you to be our baby's Godparents, and grand-parents," Charlie concluded.

Fiona's eyes went wide, and she pulled them both to her. "Oh—oh," she stammered. "Yes. Yes!"

Leona leaned into Jon and rested her head on his shoulder as she wiped a tear from her cheek.

"That's some great news," he whispered.

"The best news," Leona agreed, feeling the joy resonate through her.

"You're not going to share your news, are you?"

Leona looked up into her husband's eyes. "There's time for that later. We'll need something to celebrate next week too," she said as her husband placed his hand low on her belly where their two babies grew.

Yes, she'd tell them next week.

PLEASE REVIEW

We hope you enjoyed *The Happily Ever After Bookstore* by Bernadette Marie. If you did, we would ask that you please rate and review this title. Every review helps our authors.

Rate and Review: The Happily Ever After Bookstore

MEET THE AUTHOR

Bestselling Author Bernadette Marie is known for building families readers want to be part of. Her series The Keller Family has graced bestseller charts since its release in 2011. Since then she has authored and published over fifty books. The married mother of five sons promises romances with a Happily Ever After always…and says she can write it because she lives it.

Obsessed with the art of writing and the business of publishing, chronic entrepreneur Bernadette Marie established her own publishing house, 5 Prince Publishing, in 2011 to bring her own work to market as well as offer an opportunity for fresh voices in fiction to find a home as well.

When not immersed in the writing/publishing world, Bernadette Marie can be found spending time with her family, traveling (mostly to Disney parks), and running multiple businesses. An avid martial artist, Bernadette Marie is a second degree black belt in Tang Soo Do, and loves Tai Chi. She is a retired hockey mom, a lover of a good stout craft beer, and might have an unhealthy addiction to chocolate.

Other Titles From
5 Prince Publishing

~

The Happily Ever After Bookstore *Bernadette Marie*
The Perfect Mrs. Claus *Barbara Matteson*
The Princess of Prias *Courtney Davis*
Paige and the Reluctant Artist *Darci Garcia*
A Spider in the Garden *Courtney Davis*
Megan's Choice *Darci Garcia*
Something New *Bernadette Marie*
Something Forbidden *Bernadette Marie*
Something Found *Bernadette Marie*
Something Discovered *Bernadette Marie*
Something Lost *Bernadette Marie*
Ashes of Aldyr *Russell Archey*
Telephone Road *Ann Swann*
Paige Devereaux *Bernadette Marie*
Max Devereaux *Bernadette Marie*
Christmas Cookies on a Cruise Ship *Parker Fairchild*
Chase Devereaux *Bernadette Marie*
Kennedy Devereaux *Bernadette Marie*
The Seven Spires *Russell Archey*
At Last *Bernadette Marie*
Masterpiece *Bernadette Marie*
A Tropical Christmas *Bernadette Marie*
Corporate Christmas *Bernadette Marie*
Faith Through Falling Snow *Sandy Sinnett*
Walker Defense *Bernadette Marie*
Clash of the Cheerleaders *April Marcom*
Stevie-Girl and the Phantom of Forever *Ann Swann*